THE COLOR OF TREES

✸ The Color of Trees
a novel by Canaan Parker

Boston ♦ Alyson Publications, Inc.

Author's note

The question can arise whether a man who is both black and gay identifies himself politically as "black first" or "gay first." The question is ultimately no more than a tactical distinction. I have seen that racism and heterosexism are incestuous evils, breeding a twin-headed psychological monster, and whether one chops at one head or the other is, again, no more than a question of tactics. My enemy remains the heterosexist, racist, homophobic swine, and I dedicate this book to his ultimate demise.

Copyright © 1992 by Canaan Parker.
Cover art copyright © 1992 by Earl House.
All rights reserved.

Typeset and printed in the United States of America.

This is a paperback original from Alyson Publications, Inc.,
40 Plympton St., Boston, Mass. 02118.
Distributed in England by GMP Publishers,
P.O. Box 247, London N17 9QR, England.

This book is printed on acid-free, recycled paper.

First edition, first printing: November 1992

5 4 3 2 1

ISBN 1-55583-207-5

Library of Congress Cataloging-in-Publication Data
Parker, Canaan.
 The color of trees : a novel / by Canaan Parker. — 1st ed.
  p. cm.
 ISBN 1-55583-207-5 : $8.95
 I. Title.
PS3566.A6749C64 1992
813'.54—dc20   92-30486
                                                           CIP

My appreciation to: Pamela Pratt and all my friends at In Our Own Write, Sanford Friedman and all my friends at SAGE, Other Countries, Joe Dolins, my Apple Macintosh, and the Amazing Woodley for teaching me how to walk.

Part 1

1

We were trying to get to Green River, Connecticut, a small town north of Hartford. It had been hours since we left New York. My brother-in-law Russell was driving. Russell had lost his patience and was swearing loudly at missed exits and the twelve-wheelers thundering past. My mother sat next to Russell in the front, spying out the road signs and giving directions. I sat in the back playing tic-tac-toe with my kid brother Kenny, who was squeezed between me and my stepfather Seth.

This drive was the last I'd see of my family for some time, and there may have been some providence in its unexpected length. After breakfast we'd packed my suitcases into the trunk of Russell's blue, black-topped '66 Thunderbird and driven north out of the city, with no trouble, soon crossing the state border near Darien. By midday we'd entirely lost our way. It was afternoon now, and for hours we'd seen only miles of forest along the highway, a few farm silos, an occasional cow or horse in a field. A car had passed here and there, more often a transport truck. The big cross-country diesels infuriated Russell. One was speeding past us now, its giant hubcap only inches from our window. Russell yelled pointlessly at the driver, though not even we could hear him. When the hubcaps were past, Russell began muttering to himself menacingly.

"Somebody's buying me new tires." He reached antsily over the dashboard for a pair of sunglasses and put them on. "Somebody is buying me new tires," he repeated more loudly. "This is the last time you're going anywhere in my car. Did you hear me? The *last* time."

Russell's big mouth didn't impress my mother. "You know, Russell, if you kept your mouth shut...," she said, flipping through the folded squares of the too-large tri-state roadmap. "If you kept your mouth shut, we might be in Connecticut now instead of halfway back to New York." My mother was the only person I knew who would dare tell Russell to shut his mouth.

"Give me that map, dammit. You don't know where you're going."

"How are you going to drive and look at the map at the same time?" she snapped. She dropped the map in her lap and squinted out the window. "I'm reading the map. Turn off at the next exit."

Russell glowered at me in the rearview mirror, looking scary in his blue sunglasses. "Next time you're taking the *bus* to Green River," he shouted, and for a moment I thought he was going to stop the car and leave me by the roadside. I looked away from the mirror and out the window as we sped past the exit ramp.

"That was the exit!" my mother cried.

"Dammit!" Russell yanked off his sunglasses and threw them back on the dashboard. "DammIT!" I glanced at my brother Kenny, who was trying not to laugh.

Being lost didn't bother me at all. I was very young, all of thirteen, and this trip was exciting adventure to me, all the more so once the dwindling signs of compressed urban living — the cables of the George Washington Bridge, the moderately dense housing of the Pelham suburbs — had given way to ubiquitous country green. At one point we crossed the Rip Van Winkle Bridge in Dutchess County. I smiled to myself, daydreaming of a bony old man in a beard, and the duchess from *Through the Looking Glass*. Once we were out of range of New York City, we couldn't find any soul music on the car radio, so Russell tuned into a Top-40 station. The pop music had a different feel to it; it sounded cartoonish to me, as though the sounds were painted in primary colors and the singers all had big round eyes and buttons for noses. I thought of the silent Farmer Dell cartoons I'd watched when I was a young child, in the very early mornings before my mother arose to cook breakfast. Whenever I thought of Farmer Dell, I thought particularly of the little black cannibal, a cartoon character with a bone tied to his head, whose theme music I later learned was the *Hungarian Rhapsody* by Franz Liszt.

"Does anybody know what state we're in?" my stepfather grumbled.

"Does anybody know what hemisphere we're in?" echoed Kenny.

Seth jokingly shoved Kenny over to my side of the seat. He too was losing patience. He hadn't said much in the past hour, only piping in occasionally with sarcastic remarks to remind the front seat know-it-alls they weren't the only adults in the car.

"We could use the process of elimination," I offered. "If we cover every square mile in Connecticut, we're bound to reach Green River one of these days."

"First we have to find Connecticut," Kenny said.

Kenny and I laughed while Seth returned to looking quietly out the window.

The sun was baking the roof of the car. The vinyl seats were becoming sticky. Russell grumbled and screamed intermittently, though with waning energy. Kenny fell asleep on my stepfather's shoulder. My mother argued with Russell over whether we were going north or west. Somehow or another, maybe by luck, or maybe it was the process of elimination, we ended up on the scenic New England trail that led from Hartford to the Briarwood School, our destination.

※

This road and the surrounding terrain would later become familiar to me, yet I can still recall the sensation of newness, of freshness and birth, whenever I think of that first trip. I can only imagine, if the hills of Connecticut seemed new and strange to me at thirteen, how transcendently bizarre they must have been to Russell or Seth, who had lived their whole adult lives in New York City's Harlem. I doubt either of them had seen so many trees since leaving Georgia and Alabama as boys.

It was the very late summer of 1968, more than twenty years ago. I was going to Briarwood on full scholarship. I came from Harlem. I was born on Amsterdam Avenue on the west side; when I was two years old, we moved to the city housing projects in East Harlem, buildings that were newer and not dilapidated like the west side tenements.

My guidance counselor in my Harlem public school had told me I was an 'investment,' like a municipal bond, and as such I was especially prepared to go away to private school. I'd been exposed to the symphony and ballet on cultural enrichment field trips (that's how I identified the theme of the little cannibal). There had been classes in etiquette (the proper placement of dining utensils) and an intense program to eliminate bad diction (words like *ain't* and *git* were forever burned out of my vocabulary). I suppose you could say I was a sociological experiment.

The experiment had really begun years earlier, when my mother decided that I would embody her future retirement plan. She taught me how to read and write, choosing not to rely on the public schools. She demanded that I and all of my brothers attend Sunday School and spend half our Saturdays cleaning house. I actually had not been interested in going away to boarding school; she had made that decision, and pursued the opportunity with her usual fire. She was a very fiery woman.

She had really been to blame for getting us lost this afternoon, though in keeping with her large ego she blamed it all on Russell. Like all of us, she grew quiet as the day grew long. I remember how she stared tiredly out the window, her chin cupped in her hand. How did she feel, truly, riding through the Connecticut hills, taking her son for his first year at preparatory school? I had no idea at the time; at thirteen, I wasn't inclined to ask troubling questions. But perhaps she was wondering whether, possibly, I was being taken away from her. Another son. She'd already lost one in childbirth, and her oldest boy had died young from drugs.

Perhaps she was suspicious of all this green, all this peace. There were no wooded Edens in my mother's past; she grew up in the southern urban setting of Baltimore. She became pregnant at sixteen and married a man she described to me as "incorrigible and mean." When she was nineteen, she moved to New York with my oldest brother and sister, leaving her incorrigible first husband in jail for wife assault.

In New York she met my father, a shipping foreman at a machine parts plant. My father was a basically good man, but prone to alcoholic stupors that at their worst resembled psychosis. He was terrifically well-read for a high school graduate; I think his intellectualism challenged, intrigued, and yet bored my mother, who was tough-minded and managerial. But his income was fair by Harlem standards, and she did love him for his weirdness. She bore my father seven children and stayed with him for fifteen years, until his drinking became abominable. My mother worked as a dietary planner at a large private hospital. At the hospital she met Seth, a food services chef who went to church and didn't drink. She never formally divorced my father — she simply instructed him it was time to move out.

✺

The Briarwood School for Boys stood on a high hill, hidden from the roadway by thick, brambly woods. Cutting through the woods was a steep winding road, lined with neatly tailored bushes, that lead to the entrance to the school. We arrived at the top of the hill around sundown and went into the lobby of the school's central building, the Chase Building, where the students and faculty had already sat down to dinner in the dining hall.

Two people were seated in the lobby when we walked in — a tall, black-haired boy and a middle-aged woman in a white dress. The boy wore a blue wool blazer, a pink dress shirt unbuttoned at the collar, brown loafers, and dark green, cuffed corduroy slacks. He was sitting with one leg resting on a black travelling trunk, and I could see that he wasn't wearing socks. The woman kept bending over the boy's shoulder and whispering into his ear. He walked over and introduced himself to me: He was a freshman like myself. He and his mother had also spent the day travelling and arrived late at school. His name was Sean Landport. Sean told me that he came from a small town in northwestern Ohio and that he rooted for the Cleveland Browns. I later learned that Sean's family more or less owned northwestern Ohio, but that evening he seemed friendly and ordinary enough, and very sexy in a strange, new way. Sean and I talked about sports and upcoming courses, while our mothers commiserated about airport and highway mishaps.

Sean and I were entering the Third Form, a fancy English term for the ninth grade; there were a small number of Second Formers (eighth graders, or pre-freshmen) at school, but no First Form, which I found curious. I asked Sean about it, since he had been in private schools before. Sean said Forms were a tradition, and it didn't matter whether it made sense.

After a few minutes, a crowd of students noisily filed from the dining room into the lobby. They were almost all white boys, dressed in ties and white shirts, jackets and loafers. The overhead lights reflected sharply off their white skin, giving the room an odd glow, and it occurs to me now that I'd never before seen so many caucasian people under electric lights.

Behind the parade of students came a string of masters, and lastly the Headmaster and his wife. The Headmaster was an elderly gentleman with a swelling paunch and thinning gray hair. He wore a baggy gray suit and wire-framed glasses. He walked towards us, greeted my mother by name, and shook hands with my brother and stepfather.

My mother and I had met Mr. Chase the previous winter when I visited the school as a candidate for admission. I was nervous on first meeting him; he'd taken pains to put me at ease, so that I presented myself adequately in my personal interview. I'd sabotaged my interviews at other schools, brooding silently and crossing my arms to grip my elbows, as though I were autistic. These other interviewers seemed too brittle and formal, and dwelled on the problems I would have at their schools, coming from the ghetto, after all.

Mr. Chase, on the other hand, was enthusiastic about my prospects. On our first meeting, as he did again this first night of school, he greeted my mother by name and told her how he'd anticipated our visit. That afternoon I waited alone in the Headmaster's study, staring out the window at skeletons of trees covered intimately with coatings of frost, while the Headmaster spoke briefly with the Dean of Admissions. Mr. Chase entered the study, sat behind his large oaken desk, and asked what I was reading in junior high school. *"Wuthering Heights,"* I answered, and we discussed the tragedy of Heathcliff. There was a small lamp on Mr. Chase's desk, no brighter than a candle, which provided the only light in the room other than the snow reflection showering through the window. I could see reflections of the lamp in the lenses of Mr. Chase's pince-nez. Mr. Chase lectured me on the hardness of life at Briarwood; he sat back in his chair and shivered and squinted in an unconvincing show of sternness. His lecture was unnecessary, for I was greatly impressed, in truth mesmerized, by the finely finished oaken furniture, the candle lamplight, the crystallized shrubbery; by the Latin phrasing emblazoned on the back of my chair, and the school coat of arms that adorned trinkets on the desk and shelves — ashtrays, pewter mugs, china plates. Mr. Chase told me that my mother was a charming, intelligent woman, and that the school would be honored to assist her in educating her son.

Mr. Chase had lost weight since the winter. His hair looked thinner, and he appeared to have weathered a serious illness. He wobbled slightly when he spoke, as though he suffered from a touch of palsy. "Are you ready, Mr. Givens?" he asked, trembling with a feigned sternness that resembled choked laughter.

"Yes, sir, I think so, sir," I answered readily, having been drilled in deference and formality as part of my Harlem scholarship program.

I liked Mr. Chase, but I thought he was too fragile and gracious to survive a day at my public school in Harlem. As he talked with my mother in his soft, strained voice, I imagined him standing stunned in front of a public school classroom while packs of manic twelve-year-olds redefined the limits of bedlam.

Mr. Chase introduced me to my dormitory master, Mr. Bennett, a white-haired man with a square jaw and an impatient manner that I found more familiar — the manner of a commuter on the Times Square Shuttle. Mr. Bennett looked cool enough and mean enough to make it as a schoolteacher in Harlem, I thought. "How was your trip up?" he asked us, looking sideways, not interested in our answer. "Oh, fine. Very good," we lied.

We drove over to my dormitory and moved my belongings into my room. I said good-bye to my mother. I met my new roommate and the two seniors in charge of my corridor.

Later that evening, Mr. Bennett and his wife invited the fifteen or so freshmen on my corridor for coffee and strawberry frosted cupcakes. I sat down on the Bennetts' living room carpet and began to make my new friends.

※

There was a boy in the Bennetts' living room who stood out distinctly. His name was Thomas Adams, but he went by the nickname T.J. He wasn't a 'new boy' like most of us. He'd come to school the year before as a Second Former, so he wasn't bewildered or timid at all. He appeared to already know everyone. He was a noisy and pixieish boy, small-boned, with twinkling brown eyes. At one point he stood in the corner talking with animation to my roommate, Barrett Granger, who was also starting his second year at school.

My first reaction was that I wanted to switch roommates. T.J. was handsome and looked interesting, while Barrett was dull and looked like a llama. I resented my bad luck of the draw; T.J.'s roommate Kent Mason, a plump kid with a patchy blond crew cut, was the lucky one, I thought. Still, I was happy that T.J. and I would be living in the same house. He would be just like my brother.

My family had already left for New York. I think they were relieved to get away. Russell hadn't even left the car while he was here, and my stepfather just stood back away from everyone, tossing his keys from one hand to the other, with an unfocused glint in his eyes. Even my mother had been uncomfortable. On the corridor she put on proper airs with Mr. Bennett, speaking in the voice she usually reserved for doctors and bank managers. I'd gone into my room to unpack and left her in the hallway surrounded by nervous, blank-faced white boys lost for words to say to a black woman. I was surprised a few minutes later to overhear her in the hallway chatting away with someone, as casually as though she were in our living room at home:

"So I keep telling him, 'Turn here, Russell, turn here,' but he just keeps on going. He doesn't want to listen to me. Because he thinks he's so smart, you know. And cursing, every word out of his mouth. He's supposed to be so angry. Then I see the sign for New York City. Here he is, burning up the highway, going in the wrong direction..."

I looked out my doorway and saw the boy they called T.J. standing next to my mother and laughing. His face was flushed, his brown eyes were lit very bright. I could tell he was enjoying her story. My mother always loved an audience. She smiled her fullest smile, relaxed for the first time on this alien planet. I'm sure T.J. was the only person she met that night that she actually liked.

In the Bennetts' living room T.J. was the obvious star. He stood out like the only technicolor character in a field of black-and-white silhouettes. He was very agitated; he found it necessary to change his position every few seconds, roughly crossing and uncrossing his legs, pushing back into the pleated reclining chair he'd commandeered, then bounding up and stepping over sprawled legs and arms to find himself an empty spot on the floor. He talked more loudly than everyone, and I noticed a perpetual warble in his voice, as though his words could at any point break into nervous laughter. Though I didn't speak to him, and instead made polite chatter with a few of the quieter boys, my attention was drawn to his ever-changing location in the room.

T.J.'s room was right across from mine, so I could see into it across the hall. After the tea party, he stripped to just shorts and began to rearrange his room. He moved an easy chair to one side and hoisted a duffel bag onto the top shelf of his closet. Then he bent over his travelling trunk and strained to shove it underneath his bed. He looked up and caught me watching him. His eyes flickered, but registered nothing except frustration with the heavy trunk. He sat back and rested, winded after just a mild exertion. Then he went back to work, and his indifference to my staring I took as an invitation to continue my close inspection.

    He was thin and long-legged, slightly small for his age. He looked healthy, though not especially athletic because of his knocked knees. The muscles in his shoulders and arms were smooth and soft — all small, sweet, bulbous curves. His small brown eyes were treats — gleaming photosynthetic dots that captured more than their fair share of light. I remember that I especially liked his hair. It was cut moderately short, an inch or so past crew-cut length, and shaded a sandy brown — the color of trees. There was just enough play in the brown strands to accent the movements of his head, bouncing as he pushed, drooping over his face as he peered under the bed, and then flopping across his forehead as he reared back for a breather. With a lunge the trunk was where he wanted it. He glanced at me again, then moved to a corner, out of sight.

    I turned away and looked around my new room. The quarters were spare, almost military — two metal beds with thin mattresses and pea green bedspreads in opposite corners of the room. Two bureaus up against the wall, two spartan wooden desks right next to each other, a floor lamp in my roommate's corner, and an overhead bulb in the center of the ceiling. The walls were painted a waxy yellow. A single window looked out on a row of hedges and a white two-story house, about twenty yards back. The porch light was on and a station wagon was parked in front. I opened the window and looked and listened. There was a chill outdoors, and a breeze across my skin made my pores open. Crickets were singing to one another, their rapid, scratchy call so loud I thought a giant one must be hiding in my closet. I could see into the kitchen of the white house through a lighted window that stood out starkly in the night. From my window, I thought, I too must have stood out starkly, my blackened silhouette emphatic against a square of yellow light in the darkness.

I thought of my family, speeding on the highway back to New York in this same cool night, a little more room in the car. For a moment I felt left behind, palpably alone. I started to panic, but the sensation passed quickly. My thoughts drifted to the time when I was three years old and my mother lost me in front of the post office, and the police found me and brought me home. I could see my mother disappear into a crowd on the street, and though I don't remember speaking, I still remember a police officer kneeling down to talk to me. Oh, I also remembered being small, close to the ground — looking up at my mother's floating handbag and looking up at the seat in the police car. I was startled from these thoughts when my roommate Barrett came into the room.

My roommate was reputedly a super brain, a high honors student, which meant he was allowed to have a stereo in his room. I didn't care that he was a brain and I didn't care about his stereo. I was intuitively disinterested in Barrett. He was tall and gawky, with murky blond hair. He wore pasty-looking dental braces that slurred his speech. He didn't seem to know what to make of his black roommate; he went silently to his bureau and pulled out a t-shirt and put it on. Then he put on a record by a psychedelic rock band I'd never heard of. I didn't like rock music. The sounds were disordered and surreal — there seemed to be no start or end, no jumping-in place.

T.J. came into our room when he heard Barrett's stereo. He sat on Barrett's bed with his back to me and the two of them talked about the rock band — Vanilla Fudge, I think — and about the past summer. T.J. sat with his thigh flat on the bed. He kept running his fingers through his hair and nodding his head with animation. T.J. was still shirtless. His skin seemed to be under a spotlight — bright around the edges. He bounced his rump on the mattress and shook the bedsprings. "Your mattress is thicker than mine. Let's switch," he said. "No way," said Barrett. "Come on, Granger, switch. I'll let you blow me. You always wanted to." I was shocked to hear this and lost my breath, until I realized they were joking. The two of them looked at me, and I looked back in silence. T.J. turned away and giggled. They went on talking, ignoring me, so I sat quietly on my bed until a boy I'd met in the Bennetts' living room, Will Halpern, came in and sat down in my desk chair. Will started talking about professional ice hockey, which I knew nothing about, but his enthusiasm made it interesting. We talked until Mr. Bennett came down the corridor and announced lights-out.

2

At first I wasn't sure I liked T.J. He made me nervous. His noisy presence on the corridor was the unpredictable x-factor in my new world, and I preferred to concentrate on more orderly matters. Like obeying the rules. There were dozens of them to follow. I was always supposed to be somewhere doing something mandatory: mandatory chapel or mandatory breakfast, classes, mandatory lunch, quiet hour, then sports, dinner, study hall, a half-hour break, and lights-out. My first few days at school went by like machinework.

Mr. Bennett kept a special watch on me at first. Perhaps he thought I'd have trouble adjusting, coming from the ghetto as I did. Before long he was as brusque with me as with the other boys — abrupt commands to dust under my bed, and no excuses accepted for breaking even the most trivial rules. Mr. Bennett needn't ever have worried. I actually found solace in the strict schedules and endless requirements. Studying hard and obeying the rules were the most finite notions I had of fitting in.

T.J. couldn't abide all this regularity. He couldn't keep still during afternoon quiet hour, he couldn't get up in the morning for breakfast. He was always late on the hall after dinner. He was so different from me. I wondered if T.J. was one of those boys who suffered from abnormal blood chemistry — an oversupply of naturally occurring amphetamine.

Every afternoon was the same. "Acheson!" T.J. would call from his room in a sibilant voice that was supposed to be a whisper, but was loud enough for everyone to hear. "Acheson, can I borrow your tennis racket?"

"Keep it quiet down there," Mr. Bennett would call from his study.

"I'm sorry, sir." Then a minute later: "Acheson, did you hear me?"

"T.J., stop bothering me."

"Okay." Five minutes later, he'd come out of his room and stand in Acheson's doorway.

"Acheson, let me borrow your tennis racket."

Mr. Bennett would poke his head out of his study. "Get back in your room, T.J."

"I'm sorry, sir. I need Acheson's tennis racket."

"T.J., will you please—!"

※

T.J. made me uncomfortable, so I politely avoided talking to him, just as I'd avoided the bad boys in my public school in Harlem. But I was a fickle little puritan. Though I didn't speak, I peeked: at the suggestive scrunch of corduroy in his crotch or at the nubile curve of his bare legs and ankles. Through the corner of his doorway I could see him studying at his desk, his palm pressed to his forehead and the white glow of a tensor lamp on his face. He settled down for evening study hall and worked hard for two hours — which surprised me; I expected bad boys to be thoroughly bad, not to do their homework.

After study hall he'd revert to normal form — noisy, hyperactive frenzy. I could hear his voice from other boys' rooms and the slap of his bare feet on the floor as he ran up and down the hallway. Now I found him irritating, threatening, though no less attractive. "That boy should behave himself," I thought. "Doesn't he know this is a private school?"

At the peak of his frenzy, T.J. could be very obnoxious. He exuberantly sought out ways to offend everyone on our corridor, including Mr. Bennett, who publicly doubted T.J. would survive four years at the school. T.J. and his roommate Kent Mason patrolled our corridor as the two dominant Third Formers, teamed possessors of the most cutting wits. They threw spit wads, 'borrowed' clean towels, poured shampoo into the shoes of the more defenseless boys. T.J. concocted nicknames to suit his favorite targets: 'Femmo' Davis had regrettably admitted he liked ballet; 'Horseballs' Acheson had short black hairs growing from his nose; 'Captain Zero' suffered from an unflattering crew cut, generic facial features, and an exaggerated faith in the Republican party.

Most vulnerable of all was Ashley Downer, whom T.J. nicknamed the Frog, a sullen Second Former with glasses so thick they looked like framed shale, and whose mouth seemed as wide across as his hips. Armed with his lacrosse stick, the flaps on his white tennis cap turned downwards to resemble a safari helmet, T.J. announced one afternoon that he was going 'frog hunting,' then headed down to Ashley's room to wreak unspeakable torments.

Minutes later Ashley came walking briskly out of his room and down the hall, and T.J. right after him, waving his lacrosse stick in the air and slapping it on the floor in a zigzag pattern, as if chasing an invisible grasshopper.

"Boy, that critter sure can hop. He's too fast for me."

Ashley did his best to fight back. Down the hallway I could hear the ruckus:

"T.J., leave me alone."

T.J. answered with his frog imitation in a grainy basso profundo. "Rrrribbit."

"This is the last time I'm telling you."

"I'm trying to talk in your native language, Downer. Speak amphibian!"

"Stop it, T.J.!"
"Rrrrrribbit!"

※

T.J. reveled in self-exposure. He seemed to be constantly battling an impulse to take his clothes off in public. In the half hour we were allowed between evening study hall and lights-out, he wandered the hallway in drooping boxer shorts, the points of his hipbones bare, a narrow patch of pubic bristles showing over the stretch waistband, his penis dangling half-exposed through the slit. After showering in the morning he would linger in the bathroom to dry himself, obviously thrilled to be publicly nude.

He had a terrific gift for toweling his crotch, one foot perched up on the sink, the other on the floor, coyly concealing his cock (or was it his vagina?) so that his genital area looked bald and ambiguous. Or skillfully revealing just a few suggestive strands of moist pubic hair, his head bowed in concentrated perusal of his boyhood. Sometimes he would stand up straight and face me, looking blankly into my eyes while he stretched his shoulder backwards to dry the crack of his rear end.

I began to plan our meetings in the bathroom. T.J. must have noticed these unsubtle coincidences, and a silent voyeuristic complicity arose between us. While I, slightly stunned, stood over the toilet and stared, T.J. smiled and went on drying his crotch, or brushing his teeth in the buff, his penis jiggling on the rim of the sink in time with his vigorous brushstrokes, then sliding off and twitching gingerly in the air as he rose on his toes and cocked his head to reach his back molars. Sometimes he'd stop and stare me down or let out a little laugh.

One day I was studying geometry, and I overheard T.J. talking on the hall. "That *Givens* kid is really weird," he stage-whispered from right outside my door. I pretended not to hear him, fearing I'd end up like Ashley Downer. "Where did they dig up that *Givens* guy?" he said in a louder voice. I felt butterflies in my stomach, until he peeked into my doorway and smiled. He asked me how I was doing. "Surviving," I answered. That's all I would ever say to T.J. "Working hard," or "hanging in there."

My stone-faced responses didn't daunt T.J. at all. If I passed him in the hall, he'd poke me in the stomach or flip my necktie up into my face. It hadn't occurred to T.J., as it had to some of my dorm mates, that the black kid on the hall was 'off-limits.' He teased me like he teased everyone. But he was never really mean to me, the way he was to the Frog or Captain Zero. More and more often, from across the hall or outside my door, or in the shower, I'd catch him watching me, a mildly predatory look on his face. I became even more determined to avoid him.

※

Social life in boarding school revolved around the corridor. I became friends with the boy next door, Will Halpern, and with his roommate, 'Femmo' Randy Davis. Will was obsessed with sports — it was always football and hockey and baseball with him. He was a happy-go-lucky sort, always with a sweet, vapid smile and clear blue eyes that literally sparkled with simple, unhurt happiness. Randy was a tiny wraith of a boy with short red hair and wire-framed glasses. He liked to talk about John Locke and Martin Luther, and about different theories of morality and love. I wondered how anyone could become so intellectual in just thirteen years of life. Secretly, I thought Will and Randy were both weird, improbable people, but I liked them anyway. I didn't care that they were white — I mean, I didn't intensely feel a racial difference. I stood in their doorway whenever I felt like talking. Will noticed that I was hesitant to enter. "There goes Pete, standing in the doorway again," he'd say and, shamed, I'd enter and sit on the edge of his bed.

The Bennetts were our surrogate parents. Mr. Bennett berated us for laziness and ordered us to bed with the same exasperated bluster as any beleaguered dad of a dozen or so borderline pubescents. By corridor consensus, Mr. Bennett was the coolest master at school, partly because he was mean and selfish, and partly because his wife, though elderly, was still a beautiful woman. Mrs. Bennett could have been the ideal, stylized mom from an old TV sitcom. She was quiet and dressed plainly. She never lost her temper. And she was indeed beautiful. Her gray hair, cut short and brushed to her left, was turning silver at the cut edges. Her face was lightly powdered, her eyes were whitish blue, almost colorless; in her pastel-colored dresses she looked gracious and angelic, and sexy, even, in the way that butter cremes could be considered sexy.

On Sunday mornings, Mrs. Bennett invited pairs of roommates into her dining room for tea and English muffins. She prepared a choice of toppings — peach marmalade, blueberry marshmallow, mint gelatin — and kept our mugs filled with peppermint tea. She talked about her two sons, one at Harvard, the other in the Marines, and asked us about classes and whether we had girlfriends back home. She seemed especially fond of T.J., who became quiet and respectful in the Bennetts' dining room, inquiring about the framed photos on the divider, and mentioning that he loved the blueberry marshmallow topping, even though it got stuck in his teeth. Mrs. Bennett suggested flossing. I was touched by this gracious side of T.J., in contrast to the hysterical imp that he became every night on our corridor. I felt a fondness for him well up in my chest, and I even thought for a moment that he had changed, that his disturbing wildness was just a post-summer phase, until he saw me looking at him and knocked my spoon over into my lap. By Mr. Bennett's decree, we were allowed just an hour to impose ourselves on his family. Then he'd sally into the kitchen in baggy blue boxer shorts, sleeveless t-shirt, and sweat socks. "Get out! Go clean up your rooms!" he'd holler, and we'd scurry out and leave the Bennetts to their private affairs.

I can see, looking back, that I was a furtive little apple-polisher — ingratiating myself to my corridor master for whatever I thought I might gain. I figured Mr. Bennett liked me since I cleaned my room and didn't cause trouble. I also figured he was obliged, it was his job to be my friend. I saw him one afternoon as he walked whistling along the long path that cut from our dormitory to the gymnasium. He was wearing plaid shorts, soccer cleats, and a blue Princeton College windbreaker. His legs were surprisingly well toned for an old man with white hair. He had a coach's whistle dangling from a cord around his neck. He heard me behind him and turned just as I caught up with him.

"How do you like it here, Peter Givens?"

"Lots of work. But it's okay, sir."

"You making new friends?"

"Yes. Most of the kids seem like nice people."

"Are you getting along with your roommate?"

"He's okay," I said, looking to the ground. I followed a trail of pebbles in the path as we walked along for several yards. "Everybody's fine ... except for that boy T.J. He doesn't seem to fit in here."

Mr. Bennett paused before answering. "T.J. just has some growing up to do."

"Yes, he's immature. He's unpredictable."

Mr. Bennett looked at me with a knowing smile. Then his face showed a glimmer of worry. "Is T.J. bothering you?"

"No, no. I was just ... making an observation."

Mr. Bennett gave my shoulder a squeeze and patted me on the back. "You don't seem to be having any trouble, Peter."

"I'm fine, Mr. Bennett. Well, I'm headed over to study hall." I cut across the grass and headed for the library. I looked back to see him skipping up the gymnasium steps. I was worried, for a second, that I might have gotten T.J. into trouble.

※

Like most, or many thirteen-year-olds, I intensely desired to fit in with the boys around me. It didn't especially matter that those boys were rich, to varying degrees, and I was not. Imitation seemed the quickest route to acceptance, and so I adopted their curious preppy lingo, with its peculiarly oral taint (I took a sneaky pleasure in spouting expressions like "Eat me, Acheson" or "Ancient history really bites").

I picked up the habit of using last names. Christian names ("David" or "George") now seemed vague and superfluous, and their use even implied a genial lack of respect. It was funny to hear fourteen-year-olds addressing each other like serious, old businessmen. I assumed this was one way that prep school boys imitated their successful fathers. Still, when T.J. called me "Givens" I began to feel included.

The boys in my dormitory were all preppy, but not as I expected. Most certainly, these boys were not effete. There was an earthiness, almost a ruggedness about them, even as they walked around in their wool blazers and talked in their mannered way. They spoke of vacations in Colorado or the Caribbean or Europe, of summer homes and sixteenth-birthday automobiles, without a trace of competitive innuendo. In their world such things were really too ordinary to impress — or threaten — anyone.

Most, though not all, of the boys were "upper-middle" as opposed to undeniably "upper." T.J. seemed particularly aware of his family's status relative to the super-rich. He and Ashley would sit on the sofa in the Common Room on Sunday afternoons, toes curled in their thick crew socks, and compete not to prove who had the most money, but rather who had the least:

"Don't hand me that crap, Downer. Your family has *three* houses. We only have two."

"Bullshit, T.J. I've seen your house in Point O' Woods. All those rooms? You've got twice as many rooms all told as we do." Conversations like this left me twitching my head in confusion. It was a little hard, coming from the projects, to fathom arguments over whose family owned the *least* number of houses.

Of course, T.J. did come from a wealthy family, his populist aspirations notwithstanding. Technically, his name was Thomas Jerrett Adams III, which strikes me now as almost comically bourgeois. Yet the name fit. T.J. was the classic Connecticut preppie. He'd taken a year out of school to travel in Europe. He cut his hair short at the first sign of curls (I wished he'd let it grow longer). He dressed every day in classic boarding school garb: blue blazer and gray or pastel yellow slacks, his father's college tie, shiny brown loafers, and gray or black crew socks.

At some point I realized that my three cotton-rayon-blend sports coats, though literally conforming to the dress code, didn't really qualify as prep school style. The colorful pattern neckties I'd picked out just before coming to school now seemed garish, not sufficiently reserved. I left them in my closet, and alternately pressed and wore my two woolen jackets and my three dark cotton ties, so I could dress somewhat like the other boys. Of course, my dorm mates all had full Brooks Brothers wardrobes.

Ashley Downer noticed my limited clothing supply. "Isn't this the third time you've worn that jacket this week?" he asked me in front of Randy and Will. Ashley had the lowest status on the corridor, so I ignored him, answering only that it was weird to pay attention to another boy's clothing.

Another time we were in the Common Room complaining about the food in the dining hall. When I mentioned that my mother worked in food management and could do better, the Frog huffed in disbelief. "Your mother works?" he asked, an opaque look of surprise on his face. I couldn't tell whether he was trying to embarrass me, or really was baffled by the idea of a woman working. Everyone in the room became quiet at Ashley's remark. It was T.J. who thankfully broke the silence. "I met his mother, she's cool," he said. "She's not a useless lump of lard like you are, Downer."

Despite these occasional ripples, in not too long I was happy at Briarwood. I liked most of my schoolmates. I found quite a few of them sexy — T.J. and Sean Landport, Ethan Thayer and Mark Fix. (I kept a top-ten list of the boys I liked best, updating it weekly like a racing chart.) I also liked the masters, who seemed uniformly wise and beneficent.

And I was enchanted by the school itself, by all the green, fresh trees and grass fields, the berry-scented air. I felt enclosed by the school, by the forest ring that surrounded the campus and blocked our view of the horizon. The school was like a womb, or like warm arms in which I nestled comfortably. So quickly I'd forgotten about junkies and winos, the Black Panthers forcing their party newspapers on intimidated customers on Amsterdam Avenue. There had been the two assassinations, just a year before. Then the lootings, and the special riot police. Megaphones and mounted machine guns on the hoods of police cars. Even in New York, it had all floated over my twelve-year-old head, like smoke, but still I was aware. Now I was not aware. I was at peace, a happy, childhood peace, in my erotic paradise spanning the top of a great Connecticut hill.

3

※ The Briarwood School was not one of the great, old, mountainously endowed private schools of legend. A visitor to our school might think he'd wandered onto a country farm. The campus was flat and simply organized. The Chase Building, four stories high, was painted a faded, autumnal yellow, bordered in faded green, and covered spottily with ivy. It housed a dormitory for the Fourth Form, the dining hall, and the Headmaster's office. One narrow wing of the building housed the school infirmary, another a small library and study that we called the Common Room. Behind this main building was the school chapel, where students and faculty met three times weekly for moral instruction. Standing just a few feet from the steep edge of the hill, in the center of a spread of unused land, the chapel was the most isolated structure on campus. With its light beige brick, sharply angled wings, and very tall, narrow steeple, it seemed to gleam in a far corner of the campus like a star.

To the north of the Chase Building was a great quadrangular lawn, bordered by three red-bricked dormitories and crisscrossed by narrow paved walkways. Beyond the dormitories were tennis courts, the gymnasium, and athletic fields. Farther still were the row houses for junior faculty, brown or white wood two-story cabins with stone-pillared front steps, splintered white porch posts, white and yellow flower gardens out front, and portable grills and Volvos parked in back. On the outskirts of the campus were the large colonial homes of the senior masters and their families.

For all the oddness and newness, I was, after all, in high school. Every morning after showering and dressing, I walked the quarter mile across the main lawn to breakfast in Chase Hall, and then to class in the Petty Academic Center. My first class every morning was English, which was also my favorite. We read *The Pearl* by John Steinbeck and *Silas Marner*. I identified with poor Silas, and wondered whether my bouts of compulsive shyness weren't early signs of catatonia.

In ancient history class we read about the birth of civilization in the Fertile Crescent and the great Persian emperors Darius and Cyrus. We also learned about Hannibal, the black general who campaigned to destroy Rome, and whose legacy was Dido's vow of vengeance against the West. There were five other black students in the freshman class, and Hannibal was our hero.

I made friends with a black boy from Long Island named Keith Hanson. Keith was short and stocky and wore thick black plastic glasses. He had already decided he was headed for engineering college. He was fourteen, like me a half year young for a high school freshman, but he looked older. He shaved once a week, his baritone voice sounded almost comic as it resounded from his tiny body, and he was already growing tufts of hair on his chest and arms. Keith and I argued over the great generals as if they were baseball players:

"Do you think Hannibal could have beaten Napoleon?"

"Hannibal would have kicked Napoleon's butt. The man was too slick. He would use Napoleon's ego to trap him. But Darius would have been tough."

33

"Yeah, Darius was bad. He was African too, you know. Persia is part of Africa."

"Cyrus wasn't that great."

"Hannibal and Alexander would have been the best fight."

Keith wore an African flag pin in his tie to class every day. He wasn't very happy in prep school. He objected to calling the masters "sir," and he especially objected to having to stand up when our teacher, Dean Sanford Press, entered the room each morning. When Keith asked why our study of ancient civilizations stopped south of the Sahara, Mr. Press answered that he didn't consider himself qualified to teach the history of Black Africa.

Keith pressed him on the point. "If you're not qualified to teach history, then how did you get this job?"

The dean's face quaked, turned red, and then relaxed into a Brit-like composure. "You're welcome to do your term paper on ancient African history, Mr. Hanson. And I'll do the work to verify your facts."

Keith nodded, then turned to me with a grimly triumphant smile.

T.J. Adams was also in my ancient history class. Just as in the dormitory, he was always doing something distracting. He twitched and shifted up and down in his seat, crossed and uncrossed his legs constantly, kicked his loafers off and on. Most students were afraid of Mr. Press, but he and T.J. held a running conversation of wisecracks in most classes. The dean called T.J. "Thomas" or "urchin" or "little waif." T.J. always answered "Yes, Dean Press?" with just a touch of mockery in his voice. T.J. actually did well in ancient history. He was interested in the Roman emperors and the ancient city-states of Sumer. Though T.J. was fifteen, it was hard at times not to think of him as a little kid. I thought Mr. Press was treating him like a son.

In geometry class, I sat next to Sean Landport, the red-cheeked, dark-haired basketball player I'd met my first night at school. Sean was as tall and thin as I was, and had the perfectly squared teeth of a movie star. (Squared teeth like Sean's I assumed were the intended product of the dental braces which many of the boys wore, and which I'd never seen before.) Like T.J., Sean also called me "Givens" instead of Peter, which I liked.

Sean and I were partners in geometry class, doing problems together and combining our wits against our teacher Mr. Craig's teasing and trick questions. Mr. Craig imposed a rule that any student who complained in his class, either about unfair test questions ("jip tests") or heavy homework assignments, had to pay a quarter into the year-end spring barbecue party fund. Carter "Gorilla" Waxton, a lumbering sophomore who was repeating geometry, seemed never to get the point and was the fund's main contributor. I deliberately called Mr. Craig the all-time super jip, and paid into the party fund just to be funny. Sean shook his head and thought I was stupid. This budding young capitalist saw no humor in surrendering money willfully, not even a quarter.

On a regular basis Sean informed me that he was God's gift to women, which I didn't doubt. I liked Sean's bragging, and always tried to bait him into talking about his sex life. He wasn't suspicious, and didn't seem to notice that I didn't compete with him over girls, as most boys would have. In the locker room he demonstrated for me his bedding technique, mimicking female moans of satisfaction ("Oh, Sean! Oh, Seannieee!") while he dipped his long legs and humped his hips against his corner locker, his long red penis swirling in the air like a lariat. Sean spent his Christmas vacation in the Caribbean. When he returned I saw for the first time that uniquely caucasian oddity called a tan line, and couldn't stop laughing or staring, it seemed so odd, as if Sean had a skin disease. I suggested that next year he should tan in the nude and wrap a ribbon peppermint-style around his dick. Not amused, Sean said he would do it if I promised to suck it when he got back.

※

Parents' Day at Briarwood came in early November. It was a cold Saturday morning, and just after my second-period class I walked over to Chase Hall to meet my mother. I hadn't seen her in two months, the longest I'd ever been away. I was wearing my blue blazer and my new Briarwood school tie, hoping and half expecting to impress her. When I walked into the lobby, she looked me up and down, then her face spread into a smile.

"You should be wearing a sweater, at least," she said, brushing a speck of lint off my shoulder and smoothing down my collar. She never mentioned my daunting new boarding school manner. She just plucked and brushed, as though I were an adorably dressed doll.

We walked across to the academic center and she sat in with the other parents on my biology and English classes. In English we were reading *Henry V.* I volunteered to recite Henry's famous exhortation, hamming it up horribly to show off for my mother.

After classes there was a seafood buffet in the dining hall. Keith Hanson and his parents were there. Keith's brother Cliff had also driven up to visit. Cliff was a sophomore at Colgate University. Like Keith, he was stocky and broad-chested. Cliff liked to laugh, and had a deep, naturally loud voice. My mother mingled with the other black parents while I waited in the buffet line. When I returned with two plates of food, she was talking with the Headmaster's wife, Mrs. Chase. "He's much more confident now," I overheard her say. "He didn't use to speak at all." Mrs. Chase had a small, presumptuous smile on her face.

That afternoon was the biggest football game of the year, against the Whitehaven Academy Greycoats. Before the game, my mother came over to visit my dorm. She searched around my room like a cop, staring in surprise at my wall poster of the three TV amazon commandoes in soaked fishnet t-shirts (I'd put it up just to be cool — I didn't know yet that I didn't actually like girls). She turned and eyed me suspiciously. I could almost hear her mind clicking like a ticker tape machine, calculating silently, giving away no thoughts, but trying to figure who I was turning into.

T.J.'s parents had also come to visit. I looked across the hall and saw him sitting on his bed, his blue jacket folded in his lap. His mother was picking at his hair with her fingers. T.J. was sitting passively with a pestered look on his face, allowing his mother to fuss over him. His father, a white-haired man in a brown tweed jacket, was resting his elbow on the bureau, smoking a pipe, and concentrating hard on his boy.

Ashley Downer's father was also in our dorm. Mr. Downer was on the board of trustees of Briarwood. I knew because I'd seen his name in the school yearbook — Ashley H. Downer III, which made our Ashley Ashley the Fourth. T.J. had claimed that each generation of Downers was identical, and that they bred asexually, like amoeba. ("Who would have sex with an Ashley Downer?") I saw the two of them in Ashley's room and indeed Mr. Downer did appear to be an adult replica of his son, except that he was a very large man, and it was hard to imagine that the Frog would ever grow that big. Ashley sat stiffly upright on his bed, as though he were skewered on a beam, with both hands cupped on his kneecaps. His father seemed to be speaking in a whisper.

Just two nights before, Ashley had talked to me, for the first time really, in the bathroom as we were preparing for bed. He'd looked at me strangely while I was flossing my teeth, and asked if my parents were coming up for the weekend.

"My mother is, but not my pop."

"Why not your father?" he asked, his eyes lighting up as though he'd stumbled onto a painful secret.

"One's enough," I'd answered him flatly. He'd searched my face for hidden trouble, and, finding none, returned to applying his acne medicine.

T.J.'s mother was calling to him now from his room. I looked into the hall and saw T.J. standing with his foot propped against the wall just outside Ashley's doorway. His head was cocked. He was apparently listening to Ashley and his father. He looked up at me with an unreadable stare as his mother called again. "Thomas? Your father wants to ask you a question." He came walking back down the hall, grinning guiltlessly as he darted into his doorway. I could smell the scent of his hair, washed in oat brown soap, on the breeze he stirred up as he rushed past.

My mother and I walked out to the football field and found Keith Hanson and his parents. The six of us found seats in the bleachers and watched the game together. Whitehaven took an early lead, and the mood on our side of the field turned sour. We booed the referee and taunted Whitehaven's quarterback. Keith's brother Cliff made an extreme amount of noise, including some frat house cheers he must have learned at Colgate. Cliff thought the name Whitehaven was amusing, and he bantered throughout the game in a fiercely put-on English accent.

"Pip pip! What say we stuff old Whitehaven? Bugger off, Greycoats."

Keith was so serious compared to his brother, I thought. When Gorilla Waxton tackled the Greycoats' quarterback, Cliff went off again into his stuffy Brit routine.

"Ripping show! Sod the blooming QB. Off with his head."

My mother smiled at Cliff's carrying-on but otherwise yawned through most of the game, since she didn't know the rules or the point of football. She did get excited when Briarwood scored a touchdown to win in the final minutes of the game.

After the game we walked back to the dorm. The Bennetts were serving cocktails in their apartment just for the parents.

"Will you be all right here?" I asked.

"I'll be fine. We're going out to dinner later, right?"

"Okay." I paused and thought. "It's good to see you," I said. She nodded and smiled privately. I had an impulse to shake her hand, but didn't. I left her at the Bennetts' and went back outside. A group of about twelve Third Formers were huddled in front of the dorm, chattering excitedly.

"What's going on?" I asked.

"We're going to throw T.J. in the fish pond," said Gary Acheson.

"It's a school tradition," said Captain Zero. "When varsity football beats Whitehaven, somebody in the form goes in for a swim."

The little beast in me was instantly aroused by this idea. For a moment I felt disembodied, as my body and feelings left my thinking in the lurch. A voice usually silent spoke its piece. T.J. had teased and bothered me on the corridor. He made me nervous, and now I — all of us — were going to have our revenge.

We rushed through the doorway onto the corridor. Ashley Downer was standing in the hall. He stepped backwards suddenly as if he thought we were coming for him.

"Where's T.J.?" Captain Zero hollered.

"He's in the bathroom," Ashley told us.

We charged down the hall and grabbed T.J. as he came out of the bathroom. He started to laugh at first, until Gary Acheson ducked under his armpit and hoisted him by the waist.

"Hey, what's going on?" he said, his face turning red.

No one answered. Boys were pawing and clutching at T.J.'s arms, legs, ankles, shirttail, and collar. In an instant he was swept up horizontally. I grabbed him by the pant leg, near his thigh. I felt his warm skin beneath the cloth. Wanting more, I let go and pushed my hand further up his leg. My fingers now were grabbing his inner thigh and my wrist was tucked in his crotch. Along the base of my thumb I felt a small, tender lump, warmer than his leg, slippery. I pressed my wrist in tighter. What a hypocrite. Here I was, copping a secret feel while T.J. was getting mugged! I walked sideways down the hall with the crowd of boys, my head cocked to the side and my arm stuck into the tangle of bodies, clinging with my hand to T.J.'s leg. Ashley held open the door for us. In stumbling half steps, we carried T.J. across the quad and down a dirt path to the bottom of the hill. I couldn't see his face, just a sliver of his midsection arching up in resistance. His shirt was pulled up and I could see his writhing navel. As we neared the base of the hill his body went slack, with just an occasional jerk of his legs. We trampled a path through a patch of waist-high yellow weeds until we stood at the edge of the fish pond. Then we calmed. We turned our heads towards the rustle of an invisible animal running for cover through the tall grass. Hands dropped away from T.J.'s body until just four boys were holding him. He hung still and slack like a hammock, his head sunk into his shirt collar so that he looked like a flustered child in too large a suit.

"Catch your breath, T.J.," said Gary Acheson. Then they swung him back and forth and tossed him into the pond.

T.J. fell into the water with a resounding plop. A half second later, a spray of green water and mud droplets splattered onto the shoal.

"Agghhh! Gross!" yelled out Ashley, spitting mud off his tongue.

"What are you complaining about, Downer? Isn't this your natural habitat?"

"This is where Ashley comes for his midnight snack of flies and mosquitoes."

T.J.'s head popped up out of the water. His drenched hair was hanging to one side of his face, clinging to his ears. He dog-paddled towards us until he could stand up. Then he pulled off his shoe, scooped up some mud, and swung it at us furiously.

"Fuck you guys," he yelled, his voice warbling like a whippoorwill. He kicked off his other shoe and tossed his head to flick his hair out of his eyes. Through his disgust with the mud and the moss on his shirt, I could see he was trying not to laugh. He wiped his hands on his pants, then wiped his forearm across his mouth and plucked a soaked brown leaf out of his hair.

"You fucking assholes," he said, now smiling brightly. I smiled too, as I watched him stripping himself of wet leaves and weeds, and slapping clumps of mud off his pants. T.J. knew he deserved to get dunked, and I couldn't help admire how he accepted his just deserts with humor. No one of us was his match, and we'd admitted it with this gang attack. It had taken twelve of us in a crude show of force to achieve even this much equilibrium — an equality T.J. now dismissed with brattish laughter.

"Let's get Kent Mason," someone said.

"Only one person is supposed to go. That's the tradition," said Gary Acheson.

"Kent Mason!" yelled Captain Zero. The boys turned and ran back up the hill, screaming Indian war hoots. I walked away more slowly. I wasn't interested in dunking Kent. When I got across the patch of weeds, I heard T.J. behind me coughing. I turned and looked at him. He'd taken off his socks and shirt and was wringing out the pond water. I wanted to talk to him, but couldn't. I wondered if he knew I was the one feeling his dick. He didn't appear to know or care. I watched him for several moments, then turned and walked slowly up the hill, headed back to my room.

✺

My mother spent the night in the Bennetts' guest room and we had breakfast with the Bennetts the following morning. I was still trying desperately to show off. When she mentioned our beagle puppy at home named Caesar, I explained to Mrs. Bennett that I had named him that because he was born on the Ides of March. My mother didn't get the reference to Shakespeare, though she didn't appear concerned.

41

After breakfast, I called a taxi. We stood in front of the building and waited.

"How do you like it here, Peter?"

"Great. I like it a lot."

She looked at me keenly, still sizing me up. "Prep school," she murmured, shaking her head.

"Why do you say it like that?"

"Nothing, Peter." She took hold of my chin and looked into my eyes, searching for tears, I thought. I felt guilty because there were none. For a moment I became confused and frightened. The taxi pulled up.

"Do you want me to tell your father anything?"

"Tell him I'm fine. Say hi to Seth, too."

She got in the cab and slammed the door. "I'll be home for Thanksgiving," I said. She waved as the driver pulled off. I stood on the steps and watched as the car drove around the quad and disappeared through the bushes atop the hill.

I felt mildly ill as I watched her ride off, as though my breakfast hadn't agreed with me. There was a dull thickness in my chest, and a very slight quivering under my skin. I needed to walk, and headed towards the athletic fields. The morning had turned windy. The school groundskeepers were out cleaning trash from under the football bleachers. I walked further. A group of Third Formers were on the JV field playing a pickup game of lacrosse. Sean Landport was one of them. He had on denim shorts, the cuffs rolled up over his thighs, a black jersey, and black high-top sneakers without socks. "It's too cold for him to dress like that," I thought. I sat down on the edge of the field and watched the game. Sean saw me and waved his lacrosse stick. I waved back. I felt much better.

❋

Sean could always make me feel better. We'd become good friends by now, playing together on the JV football team. After practice every day we would dry off by the boiler in the equipment drying room. It seemed almost perversely sweet that I could stand there naked with Sean, enchanted, while he bemoaned the absence of women. Sean's body was like a bottomless ice cream sundae; I lapped and lapped with my eyes (my pleasure was just that palpable) and never got a stomachache. It didn't bother me at all that he was straight.

Sean played wide receiver on JV football, and he was a natural, with his hypnotic, long stride and big, sure hands. I had never played sports before (in New York I was afraid to go out and play), but Coach Craig was patient with me. I couldn't catch or throw a football, so I was positioned at defensive tackle, which required only that I hit people with my body.

Football was intense, though we were only pony-league level. Every Wednesday we played against rival prep schools. We'd dig up the grass with our cleats, pound our bodies together, grunt, and holler in mock falsetto fury. One or two fluttering footballs would fall by chance into someone's arms, or the defense would slip in the mud and some lucky fourteen-year-old would run free for twenty yards and score the winning touchdown. Then we'd line up and shake hands after the game, disavowing our earlier hatred. After the game I'd take a long shower, bowing my head under streams of steaming water, my body still tingling from tackles. I watched out of the corner of my eye as my friend Sean tugged off his muddy socks, wriggled out of his padded football pants, and then ran around the locker room in his jockstrap. The memory of the most solid thuds replayed itself in my nerves, the way you still feel the rock of the ocean hours after swimming at the beach.

✺

Football and classwork took up most of my time that fall. But my brightest memories of my first year in boarding school are of boys — an endless parade of boys in jockstraps, boys in basketball uniforms, boys in corduroy cutoffs and bare feet, nude boys toweling themselves to excess in the dormitory showers.

I remember mostly legs — T.J. and Sean had the best, along with Billy Green — and the golden fleshtone, a natural-looking, light bronzing of the skin that stopped short of redness and faded gently at the curved edge of the muscle to its pale, native color. In that first Indian summer, cutoffs were a delightful discovery, as were boxer shorts indoors year-round.

At fourteen, sex for me was primarily a visual affair. It hadn't yet occurred to me to *do* anything. All I wanted was to be aroused by sight of skin, genitals, and adorable faces, to express my feelings through body language — spread crotch, crossed legs, and lingering stares. And to talk, however briefly, with those few special boys with whom I fell in love. In high school I liked boys with light or dark brown hair and eyes — earthtones, the color of my own skin.

There was nothing subliminal about my homosexuality. I knew that I fell in love with boys, and I knew that I liked to look at their dicks (I hadn't yet developed an interest in rear ends). What I did not know was how to actually go about having sex with another boy. I visualized something that resembled frottage, but couldn't quite see the point of it. Knowing only the heterosexual model, my fantasies took a heterosexual form. To have sex in my dreams, I had to imagine myself as a girl, which did not trouble me or seem odd.

T.J. Adams was the most intriguing boy at school. He must have gotten wind of my queerness, because he became more aggressive in his pursuit. He stared back at me hard in ancient history class. And in the gymnasium, too; he didn't just undress me with his eyes, he put out cigarettes on my skin.

But looking didn't satisfy T.J. He wanted to talk about it. "Wow, Peter Givens in the nude," he said in the bathroom one morning, his eyes bright with pep, as I fumbled half-asleep with the rings of the shower curtain.

Another time by the urinals he shocked me with a fistful of morning hard-on, tugged reluctantly from his pajama bottoms. T.J. looked at me blurrily as he urinated, his tight, red muscle forcefully spewing piss against the back of the john while he breathed hard through his nose. When he finished, he touched the tip and his dick grew stiffer while he looked up the bathroom wall and yawned. Stiffness seemed T.J.'s natural state, his erection fueled inexhaustibly by the streams of air I could hear him sucking into his nostrils.

I must have been staring conspicuously, because he smiled sleepily and asked, "What's so interesting?" I packed up my shaving kit and hurried out of the bathroom, toothpaste still dripping down my lip.

Two days later, as I was walking towards the athletic fields to watch our home soccer team, T.J. strode up beside me.

"Where are you going?" he asked.

"To watch the soccer game." I frowned out of surprise and walked a little faster.

"You come from Harlem, right?"

"Yes. East Harlem."

"So what, are you a tough guy?"

"No, I'm not tough."

"You ever beat anybody up?"

"Not yet."

T.J. laughed, a clucking, aborted chuckle. "Oh, are you going to beat me up?"

"Probably not."

"How do you like school so far?"

"It's okay. Except it's too strict."

"You don't seem to be having any problem."

We were behind the gymnasium now, and there was no one else in sight. The path to the fields was strewn with brittle brown leaves, a few of them dancing fitfully in the wind, inches above the ground. T.J.'s hair was fluttering across his forehead. He looked at me with a soft, direct expression. I glanced at him and thought again that his eyes and hair, like my skin, were the precise color of living wood.

"You play football, don't you?"

I didn't answer.

"I've been wanting to get to know you," he said.

I started walking faster. T.J. was beginning to bother me. I wasn't sure what his intentions were, but I vaguely felt he had stepped out of line by approaching me alone behind the gym. "I'll see you later. I have to go to the game," I said. I was very brusque and rude. I stepped sideways away from him and then cut through a side path and walked the long way to the fields.

After that day I wouldn't speak to him at all. We were assigned to the same table for meals but I acted completely disinterested. He made me feel very strange. Whenever he tried to talk to me, a yellow haze would block my vision, as if I'd risen too quickly from a deep knee bend.

"You want to study for the ancient history test tonight?"

"I — No, I have to work on geometry."

"All night?"

"Yes, all night," I said indignantly. "I'm behind in geometry."

T.J.'s brown eyes flickered and went blank. "Suit yourself. Let me know when you're working on ancient history."

It wasn't guilt that turned me away from T.J. I felt my ability to respond to the beauty of boys, a beauty that surrounded me in abundance, was a private personal asset, like a box of pudding cups sent from home that I kept under my bed and wouldn't share with anyone else. It was harmless, and it felt too good to be wrong. In my deepest private world, an amorphous, nonverbal world of unasked questions and aborted thoughts, I felt that liking boys was as purely natural as the grass and the trees that populated my school so richly. I continued to play Peeping Tom with T.J. in ancient history class and on the corridor.

But I thought something like that was supposed to be *kept a secret.* That was the issue, secrecy. I was conditioned, like a spy, not to reveal such confidential matters. To be explicit, to violate the code of silence — even the thought created yellow static fields before my eyes, strong enough to blind me. And T.J. was drawing me alarmingly close to the static barrier charge between the inner and outer worlds of queerness.

4

It was obvious Ashley Downer didn't like me. Perhaps he needed someone on the corridor to have a lower status than he did. Or maybe he thought making me a target would take the pressure off him for being the class nerd.

He was too shrewd to make race the issue, at least not explicitly. My hallmates wouldn't have gone along with that. Ashley made it a question of money.

"When are you going to pay me the money you owe me, Givens?"

"I beg your pardon, Ashley?" I said.

"I'm subsidizing your scholarship. Everyone on this corridor is. What are you going to do for us in return?"

Being fourteen years old, I'd rarely been confronted with such direct hostility. I'd endured enough physical threats, of course — from the boy in fourth grade who tried to steal my coat, or the three girls in junior high who tried to take my bus pass every month. But Ashley's tactics caught me off guard.

"I think you should be working in the kitchen. Or mopping the floors. You should make up our beds every morning. It's only fair. My father is paying your tuition. All of our fathers are."

We were sitting in the Common Room on Saturday. It had been a pleasant winter afternoon, quiet and cozy, until Ashley started his tirade. Barrett Granger was there, and Kent Mason and Captain Zero. T.J. was sitting in the corner reading, one of the few times I'd ever seen him quiet.

"Say something, Givens! If you had any decency, you'd see I was right. You come all the way out here from Harlem to go to our school, and you refuse to pay your share."

"Calm down, Frogger," said Captain Zero.

"Ribbit," said Kent Mason behind Ashley's back.

"I'm serious. Don't you know what the school could do with all that scholarship money? They could hire maids. They could build a new hockey rink." Ashley turned towards Kent Mason. "I don't know about your family, Mason, but I have a maid at home. Why should I have to clean up here when there are scholarship students?"

I couldn't think of what to say. I looked around the room for support.

"I think working in the kitchen is fair for scholarship students," said Barrett.

"You guys could probably cook better," laughed Captain Zero.

"That's right. And if the Headmaster won't impose it, you should volunteer to clean our rooms. We should make it corridor policy," said Ashley.

"Frog, why don't you go lay some eggs under a rock somewhere?" T.J. interrupted. Ashley ignored him and turned his back. "Just because your father is on the board of trustees—"

"That's right. He is. And I'm going to propose it to him." Ashley turned towards me and spoke impersonally. "It's for your own good. So that you don't become confused. I've noticed lately that you've been acting confused about your background. As though you were one of us. You aren't, you know. I'm just being truthful. Your confusion could cause you problems in life."

Ashley sent a memo to the Headmaster threatening to complain to his father. The mood of the campus changed in the following days. I didn't speak to any white student. The eleven black students and the one Native American student on scholarship showed the pressure. We sat together in the cafeteria, in chapel, and in the library. Keith Hanson said we should all withdraw if the Headmaster implemented Downer's proposal. I felt awful at the thought of being forced to return home. Everywhere I went I felt like an outsider. Ashley, through his pure viciousness, received more respect from the Third Form than before. On the corridor, he glared at me with a sullen malice.

Mr. Chase called a meeting in his study with the scholarship students that Friday. He told us Briarwood was an egalitarian society, and could well afford its scholarship program, but could not afford to distract any of its students from their academic duties. Therefore no one would be required to work in the kitchen. He delivered his brief address in his usual quivering tones, beaming with beneficence as though he, at that moment, embodied the school's traditions of charity and grace. "Any questions?" he asked, smiling and quavering in his chair. Keith asked if Mr. Chase had discussed the issue with the trustees. "It's not a decision for the trustees," answered Mr. Chase.

"What about Downer's father?" asked Keith.

"I've spoken with Mr. Downer. As I said, this is my decision. Any other questions?"

When no one answered, Mr. Chase thanked us and then left the room. The twelve of us filed out of the study slowly.

"It's a good thing. I would have never stood for that," said Keith.

"It wouldn't have been that big a deal. A few nights in the kitchen," I said.

"It would have set us all apart. Waiting on them hand and foot. How could you face them in class as their servants?"

"It's over, Keith. We won."

"We'll never win from this side, brother. It's like my brother told me. 'They may let you *in*, but they will never let you *win*.'"

That night in chapel, Keith and I sat together in the choir pews at the front of the hall. There were two sets of pews that faced each other, reserved for the Second and Third Forms. After each service, the lower classes filed out of the choir pews in pairs and walked down the center aisle, leading out the congregation. Of all the people for me to walk out with tonight, there was Ashley Downer. I grimaced and hesitated. Keith gave me a shove, and I turned around to see him smirking. Ashley's face was afire. We walked stiffly down the aisle together. Behind me, barely audibly, I could hear Keith laughing in his exaggerated baritone, "Heh, heh, heh. Heh, heh, heh."

The next Saturday we were all back in the Common Room again. Ashley was stewing in a moody funk. He wouldn't just accept Mr. Chase's decision. He told me that his father would bring up the matter at the next trustees' meeting, along with a general review of the scholarship program. His eyes were beady and he looked pale, almost ill, as he spoke, shivering with hostility. "If I have my way, the whole scholarship program will be dumped."

"Fuck you, Downer," I said, having had enough.

"Fuck you, Givens."

"No, fuck you, Frog," T.J. jumped in.

"Fuck you, T.J. I'm sick of you butting into my business. Leave me alone, dammit!"

Just then Mr. Bennett came into the Common Room. "Cut out the swearing! My wife is right across the hall." T.J. apologized, and Ashley rushed out of the room.

One day the following week, T.J. caught up to me while I was crossing the quad going to class.

"I know how to nail Downer," he said.

"How?"

"That nasty little fuck. We should waste his ass."

"He's just doing it 'cause you turned him into the school clown."

"I'm no worse to him than anybody else."

"How are you going to nail him?"

"His roommate is going away this weekend."

"Acheson?"

"Make sure Acheson's going away, and let me know if he changes his plans."

Gary Acheson flew to Vail for the weekend, which meant that Ashley Downer would be alone in his room on Friday night. I made sure of this, and reported back to T.J. as he'd asked. "Fine," he said. I wondered what he had planned. T.J.'s room was strategically located right next door to Ashley's. Perhaps he was planting some kind of booby trap. Or blackmail? I would have gone along with anything to get Ashley off my back.

On Saturday afternoon, T.J. came into my room carrying a microcassette recorder.

"Listen to this."

"Oooh, Daddy. Ooooh, Daddy, I'm sorry."

"What the hell is that?"

"Just listen, Givens."

"Ooooh, Daddy. I'm sorry. I'm sorry, Daddy."

"Are those bedsprings in the background?"

"Yep."

"Is that Downer?"

"No, it's Mae West, genius," T.J. said. "Of course, it's Downer."

"Adams, I swear you are psychotic."

"I told you I'd nail that amphibian fuckface."

"What do we do now?"

"If you can't figure that out, you really are retarded." T.J. removed the cassette from the recorder and handed it to me. "Happy anniversary, darling," he said, and went out the room.

A day later Ashley Downer received a note in his mailbox. The note read, "I'm sorry, Daddy. (Ribbit) I'm sorry for sending you that letter. I'm sorry you found out my little secret. I'm sorry, Daddy (Ribbit)." We didn't hear any more of Ashley's vaunted influence with his father the school trustee.

✺

Part of me felt sorry for Ashley, even though he was a snob and a bigot. I mentioned this to Keith, and he looked at me in amazement. "People like Downer are our enemy," he exclaimed. I knew he was right, but I just couldn't find an emotion of anger or hatred inside of me.

I ran into Ashley one afternoon in downtown Green River. He was walking alone along the road headed back towards school. I was headed in the opposite direction. He was staring at the ground, absorbed in his thoughts. I don't think he even saw me. His glasses were sitting lopsided on his face. He had on a jacket and tie, and one of his shirttails was hanging out. As he walked by me, across the road, I felt oddly connected with him, as though somehow in our souls we were alike, except that I was the more fortunate.

I think that was the reason I couldn't passionately hate Ashley. We really were alike. We were both kind of weird, quiet, bookish kids. The only difference between us was race. It would have been hard for a black kid to be labelled a nerd in a mostly white school. But if I had been white, I was sure T.J. would have tortured me just as he had the Frog; or if I'd gone to an all-black school, I would have been the unpopular outcast — especially since I didn't date girls. At Briarwood I was free to hide behind the indifference of my white schoolmates. No one was looking very hard at me. And so I didn't have to look very hard at myself.

Ashley must have suspected T.J. or me of sending the note, but he never showed any interest in revenge. He started behaving out of sorts — bewildered and lost. He didn't speak much to anyone. Gary Acheson told us Ashley had become depressed. Even T.J. stopped teasing him and calling him Frog.

Later I asked T.J. how he had bugged Ashley.

"Walkie-talkies," he said. He pulled out his set of army surplus hand radios from under his bed. "I set one to send and planted it under Gary's pillow. Then I just recorded from my radio."

"But how did you know?"

His eyes flickered suspiciously. "Safe guess," he said in a near whisper.

※

T.J. and I became friends after he helped me nail Ashley Downer. I couldn't very well stay rude to him after that. And I was starting to feel like a hypocrite for shunning him but playing Peeping Tom every chance I got. After all, T.J. wasn't wrong. He was just too obvious. And not just to me. His roommate Kent Mason was spreading rumors that T.J. was queer. Of course, I had my doubts about Kent Mason, too. When Billy Green was sitting naked on the training table in the gymnasium, taping his ankles for hockey practice, Kent walked by the doorway and looked in. I swore his eyes almost popped out of his head.

One night T.J. came running out of the bathroom into my room, completely naked and dripping wet. He'd been having a water fight with Gary Acheson. My roommate Barrett laughed nervously and asked T.J. what he and Acheson were doing in the bathroom.

"Having sex!" T.J. exclaimed. Barrett just shook his head and muttered, "Jesus, Adams." I started laughing, and T.J. smiled at me, his manic black-brown eye dots twinkling under his mop of soaked hair. "What are you laughing at, Givens?" he said. He ran his fingers through his hair and spattered drops of water in my face. Then he turned and ran back into the bathroom.

"What a nut," I said to Barrett, and for the only time in the year we roomed together, we smiled.

I don't think T.J. realized what he was doing, any more than I realized how conspicuous I was when I stared at his dick by the urinals. He was just a very horny kid, his sex exploding out of him. T.J. didn't believe in self-control and he didn't believe in inhibitions. Being his friend meant I had to deal with his strange personal view of life and of the world.

Privacy meant nothing to T.J. The idea of personal barriers was as useless to him as clothing. Just by talking to him, I opened myself to a barrage of intrusions across my personal space. My appearance was now within his jurisdiction: he repeatedly suggested I grow my hair like his favorite rock star, Jimi Hendrix. "I thought you were going to grow a big afro?" he kept asking me, and I winced at the thought of myself in Jimi's frazzled, byzantine hairstyle. He could be stunningly blunt about my personal habits: "Givens, quit beating off in the shower," he hollered at me one morning. "You're wasting all the hot water."

I never saw T.J. ignore anyone, or leave anyone alone when they asked. His own nerves were radically exposed, and he couldn't abide docility in anyone else; we all had to join him in his hyperactive universe. Being quiet, egg-headed, and black, I especially piqued his curiosity, rivalling the Frog as a target of his exploratory attentions. T.J. was Dr. Frankenstein, and I and my responses were the subject of his experiments. All he wanted was to prod and test me, to piss me off or to make me laugh; to hear my jokes (few, far between, and usually not worth the wait), my problems (multitudinous), my sexual exploits (imaginary). To T.J. I was just another soul stranded on the earth, a kindred human, and therefore an opportunity for something interesting to happen.

We started to walk together to class almost every day. Since T.J. and I were both on honors, we could take morning study hall in our rooms instead of the library. Most mornings we were alone in the dormitory.

"Who's your favorite master?" he asked me one morning.

"I guess Mr. Craig," I said.

"I think Mr. Press is cool." Sanford Press was the varsity football coach, as well as our ancient history teacher and school dean. He was a big man, two hundred pounds and six feet tall, with a broad, heavy jaw and a grayish brown crew cut. It was rumored that Mr. Press had once gone through tryouts in a real pro football training camp.

"Mr. Press?" I said doubtfully. "You would pick Press."

"What's wrong with Press?"

"The Dean of Students? What if he has to kick you out?"

T.J. paused and thought. "Press would never kick me out."

"Why not?"

"He just wouldn't."

I thought of the time I'd seen Dean Press walking behind the chapel with T.J., his arm around T.J.'s shoulder. I frowned and sat up on my bed.

"You suck up to him in ancient history class," I said with a bitterness that surprised me.

"I'd like to suck up to his daughter," T.J. said. Lisa Press was a student at Trinity and spent her weekends at home with her parents. She was thin and hipless, with crystalline features and eyes that shone like blue frost in contrast to her short, black hair. More than once I had mistaken her, at a distance, for a boy.

"Let's head back to class," I said.

"Wait a minute. I have to take a piss."

"I'll come with you."

In the bathroom I sat on the sink while T.J. urinated. I looked, and his penis swelled. He turned and smiled at me casually, as if nothing were strange. "You could come home with me sometime," he said. "We could spend a weekend at my house." In the late spring of our Third

Form year T.J. meant business, while I was still just a silly voyeur.

※

In the spring T.J. offered to give me tennis lessons. Though he wasn't any good at sports like soccer or basketball, tennis was T.J.'s thing. "I'm a jock in racquet sports," he preened, twirling his racquet and flashing a rare macho pride. I figured I was destined for the country club circuit after prep school, so I agreed. I borrowed Randy Davis's racquet, and T.J. and I headed out to the tennis courts.

"Let me show you how to hold the racquet," T.J. said when we got there. He tucked his racquet between his legs and took hold of my wrist, squeezing my hand around my racquet handle. "First you have to master the swing. Don't bend the elbow. Swing with your whole arm." He stood behind me, held my elbow in his hand, and guided my arm through a swing.

"How does that feel?" he said.

"Okay."

"Try it by yourself."

I went through the motion slowly.

"No, Pete. You're—" He put his hand to his head for a moment and thought. "You're turning your whole body. Just turn your arm."

I tried again.

"You did it again. Here, let's try this." T.J. came up close behind me and tucked his finger through a loop of my belt. "Stay straight, okay, and just swing your arm." As I swung, I could feel my belt loop tugging against T.J.'s finger.

"You have to learn to feel your upper body." T.J. came up very close behind me. He placed his hands lightly on my torso just beneath my armpits. The zipper of his shorts was barely brushing against my rump. He took a deep breath and exhaled on my neck. Then he pulled me towards him lightly and goosed my behind.

57

"Stop it!" I said.

"What? I'm trying to show you something."

I turned towards him and tried to frown, but my scowl evaporated in seconds. I turned my back to him again. "Okay. Just not so close. I'm not a girl, you know."

"Christ, you're so touchy." He put his hands beneath my armpits again. "Really try to feel what your body is doing, Pete." I swung the racquet again slowly, and I could feel my torso turn and press into T.J.'s palms. "Better, better. You see what I mean."

"Yeah, I can feel my chest turning."

"It takes time. You have to become aware of all the details of your body." T.J. held his racquet out flat and started bouncing the ball rapidly, six inches in the air. Showing off for me, I assumed.

"Let's play," I snorted. "Just let me get the feel of it."

"Okay." T.J. walked to the other side of the net. "I'm going to hit it to you. Just hit it gently back to me." He bounced the ball twice on the ground, and then tapped it over the net towards me. I swung my racquet. The ball soared over T.J.'s head and high up against the back fence of the court.

"Excellent, Pete."

"I guess I hit it too hard."

"Just a little." T.J. ran back to the fence and got the ball, then ran back to the net. He bounced the ball twice again and tapped it towards me. This time I swung with great care, missing completely and falling forward on my knees. T.J. started laughing.

"Okay. Time-out. Human Anatomy 101." T.J. put two fingers up to his face. "These are called eyes. We use them for seeing. It's called the miracle of sight."

I was lying on the ground, rubbing my skinned knee. "I'd like to get you on the football field some time. I'll show you the miracle of pain."

"Don't get mad, Pete. I was worse than you when I started." I stood up, straightened my shorts, and T.J. hit the ball to me again. This time I lightly tapped it across the net. T.J. caught the ball in his hand and starting jumping up and down. "Hurray. He hit it! He hit it!"

"Shut up and hit the ball!" I said. T.J. hit the ball again. I swung and hit it. It flew over T.J.'s head, over the fence, and out of the court. T.J. fell to his knees laughing.

"Go get the ball, wise guy."

"I'll be right back," he said. He ran out of the court, searched around in a patch of tall weeds for the ball, and found it. When he came back onto the court, he was walking slowly and holding his side with his hand. He stopped and bowed his head to his chest. He started to cough. The next moment he was on his knees, coughing and choking badly. His face had turned dark red. I jumped over the net and kneeled next to him.

"What's wrong?"

He got up off his knees, tried to stand up, and then sat back down. He looked at me and shook his head. "I'm okay," he wheezed.

"No you're not. I'll go get someone."

"Give me — a minute," he said, swallowing his words. I stood up and looked to see if anyone was around I could call to. I saw no one and turned back to T.J. He was still sitting, resting on one hand. His eyes were tearing and he had turned chalk white, but his breathing was more regular. He looked at me quietly for a moment, sitting very still. "It's asthma," he said, still coughing a little. His eyes were red with tears. "I get an attack sometimes if I don't take my medication. I'm okay."

"You should take it, then," I said. T.J. got up slowly.

"It must have been those weeds. Could you walk over to the nurse with me?"

"Wait here. I'm going to get a teacher." I left T.J. and ran about a hundred yards until I came to Mr. Hays's house. I knocked on the door and his wife answered.

"T.J. is sick. He's out on the tennis courts."

Mr. Hays brought his car around and we drove out to the tennis courts. T.J. was standing there with his fingers hooked over the links of the court fence.

"How are you feeling, T.J.?" asked Mr. Hays.

"I'm okay." He wasn't coughing but still looked pale. "I need to go to the infirmary."

Mr. Hays helped T.J. into the backseat of his Volkswagen. I got into the front and we drove off. It was over a half mile to Chase Hall. I kept looking at T.J. while we rode, but he wouldn't look back. He looked all right, more annoyed now than ill. "Thanks for the lesson," I said. He winced and said nothing. He didn't speak all the way to the infirmary.

The nurse listened to T.J.'s lungs, said he was fine, and scolded him for not taking his medicine. She suggested he rest in the infirmary for a while. I had to go back and dress for chapel, so I said good-bye. T.J. reached out and shook my hand. "I'm glad you were with me when I got sick," he said, just as I was going out the door.

※

The sight of T.J. on his knees, straining to breathe, stayed with me for days. T.J. felt fine, there were no aftereffects. He went on the next day as though nothing had happened. But for me there was a change. There was a new warmth now when I looked at him, and a glow around my thoughts of him. When I watched him playing frisbee on the lawn in his bare feet and short pants, when he told me stories about digging tunnels in the snow drifts behind his home in Fairfield County, or when he picked fights and wrestled half-nude with our schoolmates on the dormitory floor, I felt almost giddy with affection. It thrilled me to think that this cool, insane kid had become my very close friend.

T.J. was intuitive, so I felt a need to be secretive about my deepening emotions. As he chattered away, I kept quiet, or avoided his eyes. I selfishly wanted to hoard this new excitement. But inside I was vibrant. My body was aswirl with pleasing sensations, good, warm feelings fluttering about inside me like crystals in a glass snow miniature, shaken up.

Oh! did he turn me on. T.J. sat in an easy chair in the Common Room and dug under his toenails, or tugged thoughtlessly at his crotch. I felt like my body was filling up with hot water. The same tumescence that was in my dick was in my arms and head and belly. I asked myself, and could think of no reason why it was wrong to feel this way.

I couldn't believe I'd ever been afraid of him. T.J. wasn't the two-legged tornado I had worked him up to be, like the Tasmanian Devil from the cartoons I loved. I reworked my romantic idealization of him: T.J. was just a boy — one hundred percent teenaged male, the platonic archetype of flushed, smouldering boyhood. Yes, he could be wild. This was how boys behaved. And I was certain now that this was what I liked.

Every day we had imaginary sex. T.J.'s body was so alive, his skin so rich and inflamed; I figured he liked sex more than anyone in the world. I dreamed of him coming — a whole-body implosion followed by jet streams of sperm that would splatter every corner of the room and could never be completely cleaned up. If only I could change (temporarily) into a girl and sneak into his room at night. I would lie on my back and raise my legs (I'd seen this position in a dirty magazine) and T.J. would mash and spear my clitoris. I would let him do anything — *everything* — to me.

In my daydreams, my vagina was a soft, mushy pit filled with fresh-picked cherries. Every night, I let T.J. crush the cherries into juice, mashing them to fluid against the wall of my clit. The shredded skin of the cherries would tease and tear at the head of his cock, or get caught inside the slit of his penis and drive him insane with an unbearable, confusing sensation. He'd scream and buck uncontrollably, captured by the need to shoot the torn bits of cherry out of the inner tube of his dick. Then he'd flood his come inside of me, washing his urethra clean of the cherry bits. Then turn over on his side and arch his body, relieved of the unbearable pleasure. I wanted to experience T.J.'s lust, to feel his orgasm as if it were mine. I wanted him to go off in my body like a bomb, to blow me to bits and splatter me in pieces on the ceiling and four walls, in every corner of the room. T.J. was my man, and I wanted him to screw my brains out.

Part 2

5

The summer after my freshman year I tried to turn my mother in to the police. We'd been on a church bus outing to Bear Mountain, and it had been a fun day. My mother had opted all afternoon for gin and sodas over grilled hamburgers and punch. When we got back to the bus terminal, she refused to give the car keys to my stepfather and insisted on driving us home. I walked up to a policeman, looked straight up into his eyes and his bushy brown mustache, and demanded he perform his duty.

"Officer, my mother is trying to drive drunk."

"What's that you said, kid?"

"We just got back from Bear Mountain and my mother has been drinking. I want you to arrest her. She's over there."

"You want me to arrest your mother?"

"Yes."

"But ... that's your mother."

"But she's been drinking."

What a nasty little Nazi I was turning into. The officer formed a question mark with his face, probably decided I was crazy and possibly dangerous, and walked away. My mother drove us home. She never said anything about my little bout of fascism; maybe she thought she'd hallucinated it all.

✹

I'd always loved and resented my mother because she was three times the person I was. She had more friends. Everyone was afraid of her. She had two husbands, and I didn't even have one. I was so different from her, so rational. At times I thought in bearing me she had evacuated all her fears, depositing them in the birth water in which I bathed, so that I was born saddled with the apprehensions of reason, while she was left free to roam her territory, conquering men, like Shakespeare's inflamed, regal stallion, *her ears up-pricked, her braided, hanging mane...*

It wasn't fair. I felt I had been formed as her opposite, created to be her opposite, and I felt cheated of my genetic inheritance. Whether, in her garrulousness, she left me no room to grow comfortable with my own voice, or whether, like Dido, it was her instinct to dominate all males, whole regions of my person were squashed. She filled the living room with her expanding presence; the only space left to me was in the corner, cowed and numb, never heard.

At boarding school I was free. The culture of reason and pale puritan elitism offered to vindicate me in my silent battle with my mother. I can see now that I overreacted, that my receptivity to the traditions of Briarwood was heightened by Oedipal stirrings. (Can a gay boy have an Oedipal complex? Can a woman have a Napoleonic complex? I'll leave it to strict Freudians to drive themselves crazy pondering what for me is the obvious answer.)

If my sojourn in Connecticut was a sociological experiment, then no one had figured how my being gay would skew the lab results. My education took a surprise Pavlovian twist. The boys at Briarwood became symbols of my school's traditions — discretely European traditions — in my subconscious mind. They were tough and earthy and gracious. And filthy rich, of course, but the musk of their aristocracy was as slight as the scent of berries on a summer wind, so subtle it did not offend — did I actually smell it? Was that my imagination? The taste of odorless gas on my lip is the only evidence of mind surgery. I awake to the sight of Sean Landport's milky cock, by now my private friend, peeping out from the slit in his boxer shorts before he roughly tucks it away, brusquely zipping up his Brooks Brothers cords. Until tomorrow. Then the sight of his buns again, the next afternoon, and T.J.'s and Billy's and Ethan Thayer's — the rhythm of stripping and toweling and zipping formed a carrier wave, and on that wave was a coded inducement to treason.

※

Certainly, I wasn't sent away to school to be turned into a traitor who could turn his own mother in to the cops. And I'm glad to say that didn't happen. For all my failings, I certainly have turned out a better person than that. But I might not have. My salvation came in the most improbable form — a queer little two-legged hurricane who insisted on reminding me that I was human, after all. A fact I was trying to ignore.

It all comes down to the truth. And the endless convolutions we concoct in our minds in order to resist the truth. I wanted to believe that the secret of life was the will. That manna would flow in direct proportion to my willful exertions, under my direct control. Work hard and succeed — the equation was just that simple. That this thing called my body would interfere, would do what it wanted or had been shaped to do, or born to do, I thought the ripest heresy. That I was bound to my family, and through them to a race of people, and had no say in the matter, that *other people* could impact my life through their actions and weaknesses — these facts infuriated me. I felt trapped by biology, and I resisted the idea with a dogmatic's ritual panic.

T.J. was my link to the truth. His mania, his visceral explosions were glimmers of truth away off on a dark sea, faint beacons. My journey to light would be hard, I would turn back many times. Even now I can't be sure that I've made it.

If I was ultimately saved from a life of psychic fascism, then who can tell what emotional horrors I've been spared. Traces of fear do linger. Flashbacks of emotional barrenness from time to time invade my dreams. That may be the reason I'm writing this book. To reinforce my salvation, to keep myself from slipping back, from turning back into that frightening, doomed fourteen-year-old, tugging on the policeman's coat.

6

☀ For all his impish ways and provocativeness, T.J. was a bright and serious student. He got to know me by studying with me, first ancient history in our Third Form year, and then trigonometry in the Fourth Form. In the Fourth Form, T.J. and I lived on different floors in Chase Hall. He came to my room during study hall often, usually shirtless and barefoot. I sat in my easy chair and he took over my bed as if it were his own, wrinkling my blankets and twisting his body into assorted angles and positions. One spring night he seemed particularly agitated.

"You want to come home with me?"

"What?"

"Come home with me. For a weekend. You want to?"

T.J. had caught me by surprise again. Sophomores were allowed one weekend off campus each term, and T.J. was suggesting he and I take a weekend together.

"Sure," I muttered.

"'Sure,'" he mimicked. "You're such a twerp, Givens. It'll be fun."

We were studying for our spring trigonometry midterm. My grades were a bit better than T.J.'s (I just passed the cutoff for high honors and he just missed it), but in mathematics we were equals.

"I can't wait until this fucking test is over." He slammed his math book shut and tossed it in my lap. "You like this stuff, don't you? Sines and cosines. You probably beat off thinking about angular velocity."

"I just want to beat Barrett Granger's ass."

"I'm starting to hate this fucking school." T.J. bit his lower lip to exaggerate the *"f"* in "fuck." He screwed his body up into an impossibly contorted position. *"Fuck* trigonometry," he said loudly, his breath whistling between teeth and skin.

We were both young enough that just saying dirty words gave us erections. T.J. reminded me of my little Puerto Rican friend Louis from the fifth grade, with whom I'd discovered swear words at age ten. Louis and I would curse each other chummily, tickled by the wicked-sounding consonants. Instead of saying hello, we'd greet each other with "Suck my dick," and laugh. We'd wave good-bye and say "Fuck you," instead of "So long" or "See you later."

T.J. flopped backwards on my bed and stretched out his legs. He kicked me in the thigh and smiled, then rested his ankle on my knee.

"Why are you so weird, Givens? How come you're such a queer? How come you've never been laid in your life?"

"At least I'm not a fairy in women's clothing." He kicked me again and threw a paper clip at me.

When we were Third Formers, T.J. loved to bother me — he called it "giving me grief" — because he knew I wouldn't respond verbally. I couldn't compete with T.J.'s sparkling lunacy. I'd act calm for as long as I could, then grab him by both arms (his skin was always hot) and order him to leave me alone, but he'd only giggle crazily, egged on by our physical contact, and I'd end up punching him in his chest to shut him up.

By our Fourth Form year, his lust for me had grown into affection. I was still quiet and he still insulted me, but with a lighter touch, and I grew more confident and more fun for him to be with. He went out of his way to spend time with me now, studying in my room or playing basketball with me on Saturday nights.

"So you want to come home with me?"

"Definitely," I said. "Next weekend, after the test."

T.J. jumped up off the bed, grabbed his math book from my lap, and went out the door.

※

The next Friday afternoon T.J. and I took a taxi into Hartford and then the train from Hartford to Old Greenwich, Connecticut. His mother met us at the railroad station. "Hi, Tom," she beamed, standing up on her toes to kiss her son. Mrs. Adams was a small, attractive woman in her middle forties. Her hair was black and done stylishly. She looked well conditioned in a pink jogging outfit.

"Hi, Mom. This is my friend Peter Givens. He's spending the weekend."

We got into a green Volvo station wagon and drove a mile or so parallel to the railroad tracks, then over a bridged river and several miles of narrow, winding road through what seemed an uninhabited forest. T.J. talked to his mother about her tennis match, which she had won. ("Do you play tennis, Peter?" "No, ma'am.") Houses began to appear, then light auto traffic.

Mrs. Adams turned sharply into the driveway of a two-car aluminum garage. To the side of the garage was a wall of seven-foot hedges. T.J. led the way over a crooked cobble pathway through the opaque greenery. Several yards into the brush was a gravel clearing, and then a great wide lawn that dipped downwards. Ahead I could see a bright yellow house, holding perhaps ten rooms, with black shingled roofing and black framed windows. We walked around to the side of the house and entered through the glass doors by the patio.

"Where's Dad these days?"

"Your father is in Chicago on the Bodner project, you remember. And I will be joining him tomorrow morning. So you kind boys please don't destroy the house while I'm away." T.J. turned to me and grinned, freezing in his steps for a moment as though he'd had a mild cataplexy.

Inside the house, the main visual theme was varied shades of brown wood — wall paneling, uncarpeted floors and stairways, ceiling crossbeams, dark polished furniture. T.J. and I went upstairs to his bedroom and dropped off our carrying bags. I sat nervously on the corner of his bed while he changed his clothes.

"I love weekends," said T.J. "The only thing Briarwood is good for is vacations and weekends." He had stripped to his undershorts and was searching through his bureau for something to wear. He pulled a pair of blue jeans out from under some sweaters and put them on.

"What's wrong?" he asked.

"Nothing's wrong."

"You're acting a little nervous. You want to hear some music?"

"You mean that hillbilly crap you like. No thanks."

"Sorry I don't have any stinking soul music."

"It's weird to hear your mother call you by your real name."

"Everybody in town here calls me Jerrett. But my father's name is Jerrett, so my mother calls me Tom. But at school they call me T.J."

"It must get confusing."

"Not really." T.J. slouched back in his desk chair and knotted his fingers across his stomach. "I'm hungry. Let's go down and eat, Pete." We got up and went back downstairs.

We had steak and french fries for dinner in a very large and old-fashioned dining room. T.J. shoveled food into his mouth while Mrs. Adams interrogated me about growing up in New York.

"Pete's really smart, Mom. He's number two in the class. But that's just because he brownnoses all the masters."

"And Barrett Granger is still number one?" she asked.

"Granger is a jerk," I opined.

"I'll tell him you said so, Pete."

"Go ahead."

"Don't forget to fill your prescription tomorrow, Tommy."

"Sure, sure." Mrs. Adams stared blankly at her son for a moment, then smiled dearly.

"Well, I have to rest tonight. My plane leaves at seven, so I'll be gone when you wake up, probably. Where's Peter going to sleep, Tom?"

"I'll move a mattress into my room. Okay?"

"Okay. Just put it back, please."

"Sure, sure."

"Yes, sure." She turned to me. "Peter, you'll make certain Tom doesn't burn my house down, won't you?"

T.J. put his hand on his mother's wrist. "You're kind of obnoxious for a parent, you know that?" She pulled away and slapped his hand sassily and got up from the table. I thought again of how T.J. made my mother laugh the first night I met him.

"Good night, Peter."

"Good night, Mrs. Adams."

"Good night, Mom."

"Good night."

I decided T.J.'s mother was a cool person and a genius at raising kids. She'd given T.J. the leeway to develop his manic personality and still imbued him with values of hard work and integrity. And she loved him dearly, totally. I could tell.

T.J. and I watched television in the study and went upstairs around eleven o'clock. We dragged a mattress and bedspread from a guest room into T.J.'s bedroom. T.J. kept pressing his warm torso against mine and smiling while we moved furniture around to make room for the mattress.

Then we lay down on our beds and talked. T.J. did most of the talking, as always. His words triggered my free associations, and my mind wandered, half-attentive, over thoughts of tennis matches, the railroad station, the teenaged girl who kept looking at us from across the railroad car. T.J. prattled away in his soothing tenor.

I curled myself in my bedspread and listened to the sound of French horns that was hidden in T.J.'s voice. Most of the white kids at school spoke with some element of that sound, a slight brassiness buried in the overtones, something unique in the construction of the throats and chest cavities of young caucasians. In T.J., the horns were especially shiny and golden, the tone somehow both smooth and sharp.

"So what's it like living in Harlem? It must be pretty tough."

"I didn't think it was that horrible. I was used to it when I was living there. Now I can see it's pretty bad when I go back."

"Tell me some ghetto horror stories."

"Well, let's see. Once I saw this drunk guy beating his wife in the street with a chain. My mother got robbed by a guy with a knife. Some guy pulled a gun on my father once. My father came upstairs and got a knife and went back after the guy. I thought he was going to get shot. I mean, what good is a knife against a gun?"

"Jesus, Givens. I'm glad I don't live in Harlem."

"Once I was over at my sister's house at night. And the door started rattling and shaking like someone was trying to break in. My sister screamed — I'm telling you, T.J., you never heard fear in a person's voice like this. It was pure human terror. But it was just my brother-in-law. He was drunk and he couldn't find the lock."

"Jesus."

"Once my brother-in-law and I caught this Puerto Rican guy in his apartment. We opened the door, and this guy was right in the living room. My brother-in-law chased him down the fire escape, but he got away. Just imagine if it had been me and my sister instead. We'd both be dead, right?"

"Yeah. That guy would have definitely killed you. Jesus." T.J. was lying upside down on his bed with his feet propped up against the wall.

"So now you're an Oreo," he said.

"What?"

"An Oreo cookie. White on the inside and black on the outside."

"What color is my skin, T.J.?"

"Black ... brown?"

"It's black. That's all there is to it. I'm black."

"But on the inside you're white. I think you're whiter than I am."

"Fuck you. Where did you get that expression from? Oreo cookie."

"From your friend Keith Hanson. He was talking at lunch about Oreos — black traitors. He's really radical."

"That's his opinion. He's not exactly the head of the Black Panthers, you know."

"I guess I'm pretty lucky to be rich. But we're not really rich. We're just comfortable. You know, secure."

"What does your father do?"

"Fuck if I know. He works for a bank." T.J. spun his legs around, got off his bed, and disappeared downstairs for a minute. He brought back two cold bottled Coca-Colas and sat cross-legged on his bed once more.

"Do you like it at Briarwood?" he asked me.

"Yeah. I like playing sports. The work isn't that bad."

"There's no girls, though."

"Yes. That's a problem." T.J. and I still towed the party line on girls, even though we'd implicitly agreed a long time ago that boys were more interesting.

"I'm not that happy at school."

"What's wrong?"

"Well, I have, you know, this reputation. Everybody thinks I'm an asshole. Everybody in the whole school, even the faculty."

"That's why we threw you into the pond."

"I still haven't gotten you back for that. But I will, don't worry." T.J. didn't realize it, but I respected him for being able to provoke people into throwing him into a fish pond. I could never motivate a group of people like that.

"I'm thinking of transferring to another school, just starting all over again with a new identity. Make some new friends. I couldn't even find my own roommate. It's embarrassing when they have to assign you some jerk of a new boy for a roommate."

"Why didn't you room with Kent Mason again?"

"I got sick of him."

"Last year he was telling people you were turning queer on him. He said you were getting queerer by the day."

"Who cares what Kent Mason says? Nobody likes him. He's a depressant." T.J. took a long swallow of his Coke. "I thought you and I might make good roommates."

"You should have asked me."

"I did ask you, sort of."

"When did you ask me?"

"Well, I didn't exactly ask you, but I dropped a hint. You just didn't get it."

I remembered the day in the Common Room when T.J. asked who I'd be rooming with next year. At the time I thought he was just being curious. I frowned now at the opportunity I'd missed.

"What's wrong?" he asked.

"Nothing."

"There he goes into fogland again. I'm sorry to have to tell you this, but you're not the quickest guy in the brains department, Pete."

"Tell me all about it, T.J."

"No kidding. I've got you all figured out. Your brain is totally conditioned by tests. As long as somebody asks you a direct question, you can give them the answer. But if nobody asks you a question, your brain just sits there, like a blender or something, waiting for somebody to turn it on. So most of the time — like in life — your brain just sits in neutral."

"Thank you, Dr. Freud."

"Anyway, I didn't think you wanted a honky for a roommate."

"Why not? Where are you getting these expressions from?"

"I'm kidding. I know you wanted a single room so you could beat off in private."

"Leave me alone. I'm going to sleep."

"Now he's going to tell me he doesn't whack. I know you whack off, Givens. I heard you moaning in the closet on Bennett's corridor."

"Good night, Tommy."

"Hey, Pete."

"Good *night,* Tommy."

"Pete!"

"What?"

"Tomorrow's your lucky day."

"What's happening tomorrow?"

"Go to sleep."

※

In the morning T.J. and I took the Volvo into town to shop for food. Then we stopped at the pharmacy. I waited outside while T.J. picked up his asthma medication and surveyed what I could see of the town.

In ancient history class, we'd learned about the Fertile Crescent, a strip of land in the Middle East accredited with the birth of civilization. I liked the sound and the idea of the Fertile Crescent; I'd appropriated the title as a nickname for

Old Greenwich, which on a per capita basis had produced by far the highest number of Briarwood's cutest boys. I couldn't believe I was now actually standing on the modern Fertile Crescent. So many sexy boys come from this town, I thought to myself. Mark Fix, Billy Green, Tim Rainier. And of course, T.J. And boys I hadn't yet met.

The town's very small shopping area was deserted; it seemed ordinary, like any town, a pocket of middle-class familiarity that might mislead a misplaced traveller to think he was in an average American village, though I knew better. I inspected what I could see with affection for this fertile wellspring. From where I stood, the right angles of the nearest intersection appeared to shear into a distended X. To the east, the street vanished into rising sunlight. In the distance I could see a long grass hill spanning the horizon; beyond it, the Connecticut interstate. Miles off, the sun gleamed off the tops of automobiles floating rapidly across the view, in silence. I could hear only birds chirping their morning ritual song. Their call, sweet and precise, and emboldened by human absence, echoed in my eardrums as though its source were only inches away. To the south and behind me, to the west, about a hundred yards off, the street slipped into shadows under thick tree brush — a color scheme of dark greens and black — and disappeared around wooded corners into the privacy of wealth. I wondered about the boys who lived beyond those curves — their late-evening thoughts, the troubling secrets that might even make them cry at night.

T.J. came out of the drugstore smiling brightly, his tea-colored eyes absorbing light and firing it back (his special gift for ocular photosynthesis). "Let's go, Pete." We drove back to the house and cooked french toast and bacon for brunch.

T.J. gave me a pair of his shorts to wear, and we went swimming in the backyard pool. We made roast beef sandwiches for lunch, and watched a tennis match on TV while our bathing shorts dried. I was a little bored, but T.J. got up close to the screen and commented on the players' tactics.

Later he showed me around the house, pictures of his mom and dad and his older brother Jeff, a freshman at Harvard. T.J. had changed into blue jeans, unfastened and half-unzipped, that drooped an inch or two over his bare hips and hung too far over his heels, scuffing on the floor when he walked.

"All right, Givens. There's one rule you have to follow in this house. No clothes after sundown."

"What?"

"No clothes. No pants. It's warm enough in here."

"You're kidding, right?"

"I'm not kidding. Take your pants off." He started to laugh.

"Wait a few minutes." T.J.'s scuffing blue jeans had given me a hard-on.

"Not later. Now." T.J. was giggling now, revving up to hysteria as I'd seen him do so often. He pushed me backwards a step, then started flipping the underside of my dick through my shorts with his fingertips.

"What's this, Givens? A boner with no girls around? You're not *queer*, are you?" T.J. was fully hysterical now: giggling and grabbing at me, skin flaring, breathing audibly and bobbing his head. A foot away from me, I could feel his body like a pot of boiling water, bubbling and popping, pouring off warm steam. He grabbed the band of my shorts and wrestled them down over my hips. My dick flopped out.

"You're not the only guy in town with a boner on," he said, reaching down into his crotch. He needed his full hand to tug his erection out of his pants. It fought back for a second, then snapped out of his jeans. I looked away.

"Don't worry about it. It's natural," he said, kicking his way out of his jeans, the head of his dick cutting lively figure eights in the air. "You never worried about it before." He frowned as if my dumbshow of surprise was too absurd even to be funny.

We sat down on the edge of his bed. T.J. snapped the head of my dick with his fingers like he was shooting marbles. Then his, then mine again. "It's fun, right?"

"Why do I have to take my clothes off?"

"Are you complaining?"

"No, just wondering."

"Because I'm going to fuck you, that's why."

I didn't know what he meant.

T.J. shunted back against the wall behind his bed. "Don't you know about the new sex? You shove your dick up the other person's ass. It doesn't matter if it's a girl or a guy."

"You're crazy. It couldn't fit."

"It goes in if you push hard enough."

"I don't think I want to try that."

"Just keep thinking about it," he mused, as if speaking from experience.

T.J. ran his fingers up and down my dick. "Let your fingers do the walking..." He slapped his penis back and forth against his belly, then lightly drummed his fingers on my testicles.

"What if I took your nuts and twisted them around like this?"

"Your mother would find your dead body when she comes back, that's what."

"You don't know anything about sex, do you?" he asked smartly. "You never been laid, you don't give ass. I bet you don't even know what a blowjob is."

"I know what a blowjob is."

"I really like black lips. They're so thick and smooth." T.J. put his arm around my shoulder. I started to feel nervous and dizzy, as though my mind were dissolving. My eyes kept blinking shut involuntarily. I knew what T.J. wanted. I had never thought of actually doing something like this. But I felt it was fraudulent and disrespectful to

T.J. to resist him, since I'd enjoyed the sight of his naked body so many times. I felt I should repay him for all the visual pleasure he'd given me.

"I wonder how it would feel if I put my dick in your mouth," he said. I was shivering now. I sat very still and looked ahead.

"Come on, Peter. Can I do it?"

Without waiting for an answer, T.J. jumped up on the mattress and straddled my face, poking me in the nose with his boner. He pushed my head against the wall with his pelvis, then slipped his fingers behind my head to keep me from bumping against the wall. He slipped his dick in and out of my mouth. The head tasted smooth, like a marshmallow, but the shaft was thick, meaty, like cow's tongue. As he pumped in and out, he said the same syllables over and over, as though reciting practiced lines: "Ooooh. Ssssss. Ahhh. Ssssss. Oooh. Sssss. Ahhh. Ssssss."

I felt as if there was a warm light behind my eyes, as if I were taking a warm shower. T.J.'s stomach felt like a glassine bag filled with hot water. I sniffed, then deeply inhaled the aroma of his fresh pubic hair. I scrubbed my nose in the bristles and plugged my nostrils with the head of his dick. T.J. stopped pushing his pelvis forward. He stood still, moaning softly, his head pressed sideways against the wall, his legs bowed like a buddha's. I was now sucking happily. I felt in a surreal place, lost in a wonderland of wetness and heat. This was so new. Nothing had ever been so new as the marshmallow sweetness of T.J.'s dick, or the furry, sagging weight of his balls, now giant boulders blocking my view, bouncing off my face and dragging across my eyelashes as T.J. pulled out and lost his balance for a second. He fell forward, stepped on my thigh by accident, and apologized. Then he flopped down next to me and started nuzzling around my neck.

"You want to try that ass thing?" he asked.

"I don't think so."

"That's okay. That blowjob was enough. You can really suck dick, Pete. You're a natural."

"Now I know why they call it meat. I felt like I was eating a hero sandwich."

"It's a good thing you had lunch first. I'd better remember to feed you before I fuck your mouth again."

We sat quietly for a while. I rested my head on T.J.'s shoulder and fell asleep for a moment, then snapped back awake. T.J. had one hand tucked behind me, near my ass, and was teasing out my pubic hair with the other hand.

"You're getting sleepy, huh?"

"Yes."

"Just rest. You deserve it." I lay my head back for several minutes while T.J. continued to play with my dick and comb out my hair.

"Do you want me to blow you?" he asked.

"Sure." T.J. got up on one knee and sucked me tenderly. This more familiar sensation also felt wonderful, though not as good as when I was sucking T.J. T.J. was straddled awkwardly across my leg, and I bent my knee upwards and caressed the crack of his ass with my kneecap. He turned more awkwardly so that my knee fit more snugly, now practically crawling over me like a crab, still sucking and jerking himself off until he splashed come on my belly.

A look of disorientation flashed across his face. He sat down next to me against the wall, one hand on his thigh and the other on the sheet. I leaned towards him, twisted against his chest, and pressed my face against his nipple. We sat like this for a while. T.J. didn't speak for several minutes. Then he moved in front of me on the bed and sat facing me.

"If you were a girl, would you let me fuck you?" he asked.

"Yes," I said without hesitation. I thought he'd read my dreams.

"I'd let you fuck me if I was a girl."

"Did you ever fuck a girl?"

"Yeah. They make a lot of noise. I fuck this girl in town. She's hot for my nuts. She's been hot for my nuts ever since I was in Day School. Her name is Dolly. Her pussy is a mess. All mush and slop. It feels like hot water on my dick. She wants me to eat it, but I won't. I'd throw up if I ate pussy." He paused. "I like you better than her."

"It's too bad I don't have a cunt."

"Think about that new sex. Then it won't matter."

※

T.J. let me have the window seat on our trip back to school (a critical issue to adolescent boys). I rested my head against the glass and studied the woods and rails as the train rocked slowly northwards to Hartford.

It was late Sunday afternoon and the sun was setting below the tops of the trees. I imagined the sun and the forest were fencers; the plants had the advantage and parried the majority of solar thrusts. An occasional lancing score of gleaming orange broke through the trees, blinding me temporarily and radiating the inside of the railroad car. I wondered what adventure I might find if I could change the vector of my motion and explore pathways right-angled to the railroad tracks deep into the shadowy, tangled green, which seemed now more like Nigerian jungle than New England wood.

I felt exhausted and permanently altered, as if I'd received fatal news from the hospital. The world was different now. I'd crossed the line into gay sex, and though my boyfriend (my husband) was wonderful, I still felt drained and anxious. T.J. pressed his knee against mine and left it there. My body was his now; he could do what he wanted. He smiled and I misplaced my anxiety. I reminded myself I couldn't rest my head against his shoulder in public (I accepted this, though it made no sense to me). T.J. talked all the way from New Haven to Hartford. My head was buzzing, though, and I heard only half of what he said.

We got back to school around eight o'clock and checked in with Dean Press. As we walked towards our dormitory, I thanked T.J. for inviting me to his house. "My pleasure, Pete," he said.

Later that spring, the school held a Seminar Day, and one of the seminars dealt with black culture. T.J. picked that seminar, and came dressed like a real Fairfield County prep, wearing his white tennis jersey, blue jeans, and loafers with no socks. He asked silly questions: "Is there really that much difference between soul food and regular food?" He wanted to know about black people and black America. Nothing could have made me want him more. That night I offered my brown, honey ass to him. He fucked me like a wild pony and coated my soft, black rectum with his preppy seed.

*

As fond as I was of T.J., I was not infatuated with him. My first infatuation at Briarwood was with a boy in the Fifth Form named Cady Donaldson, who played with me on the JV football team. We played our first game against the Gunnery School, whose school color was red. As we did our jumping jacks before the game, we shouted in rhythm that we were going to "Eat Red Meat." It was a murky, windy fall afternoon. Midway through the second period, Coach Craig sent a substitute into the game to play beside me on the line. The reed-thin boy, teetering beneath his shoulder pads, tapped me on my shoulder and asked in a pinging, nasal voice where he was supposed to play. From inside his football helmet, Cady's gray-blue eyes sparkled at me and seized my breath. His eyelashes were long, and his narrow, black eyebrows stood out in stark contrast to some unspecified point of reference. I fell in love instantly with his eyes, which shined like silver laser beams.

My infatuation with Cady was bizarre and hopeless. We never spoke to each other, communicating solely through eye contact across the dining room or at football practice or in the hallways of the academic center. I invented vicarious ways to connect with Cady: I imitated his quick, side-swaying walk. I drew pictures of him in art class. During the summer, I studied roadmaps to find Cady's hometown, a small, rural village in northern New York State. Looking at the tiny dot on the map, I imagined that I could be with him, perhaps go pony riding with him on the giant spread of farmland his family owned.

While working on cleanup detail, I sneaked a look at Cady's confidential file in the Headmaster's library. Cady had come to Briarwood as a Second Former. Though his grades were fair, his IQ score showed he was still an underachiever. He'd become erratic and depressed in his first year. In counseling sessions he'd admitted he missed his Red Setter puppy "Roxie" at home.

In the springtime of my sophomore year I got to know Cady's best friend Kelly, who looked uncannily like a girl and wore dungaree shorts cut just barely below his genitals. He called them his "faggot hot pants." Kelly and I were on the track team. He did the high jump and I ran hurdles. We always sat together on bus rides home from away track meets.

Although he was only fifteen and came from a small town, Kelly must have been exposed to an openly gay scene at some time, I think, to become so girlish. He had been in boarding schools since he was eleven years old. He received a new stereo for his birthday, and he invited me to his room to listen to records. Kelly loved the Beatles and the Alice Cooper Band. He was dancing to Alice Cooper when I walked through the door.

"What's happenin', man?" Kelly thought it was cool to hang out with the black students and to mock our way of speaking. He bobbed up and down and shook his hair as Alice Cooper screamed out hard electric riffs. "Man, listen to that guitar." He had on his faggot cutoffs and white, low-top sneakers with no socks. I couldn't keep my eyes off his long legs and bare ankles.

"What are you looking at?" he asked.

"Nothing, Kelly."

"Nothing, huh? That's okay. You don't have to tell me. 'Cause I already know." He smiled. My voice was naturally soft, so I had trouble talking over the music. Kelly turned the speakers down and led me by the wrist to his bed. We both sat down. He leaned back against the wall, put both feet up onto the bed, and crossed one leg at the knee.

"Pete, you're cool. I like you. You're quiet but you're cool. I've got plans for you, Mr. Givens."

"Oh, yeah? What kind of plans?"

"Go turn the music back up and I'll show you," he said as he jumped up to lock his door. I walked across the room to Kelly's stereo and he followed a couple of steps behind me. "We gotta cover the noise," he whispered.

Kelly wrapped one wrist behind my neck, standing arms' length away from me, and with the other hand unbuttoned his shorts and shunted them down over his hips so they fell to the floor. He lay back down on his bed, naked except for his sneakers, and threw his legs up and over his head. Though his legs were skinny, his ass was wide and round, like fat white melons. He tucked the heels of his sneakers behind his neck like a contortionist. His ass stood up like a separate, living entity, and his head appeared disembodied, encircled by his skinny legs.

"Come and ball me. I'm helpless."

I'd been thinking about doing this ever since T.J. mentioned it. I jumped out of my clothes and slammed into Kelly as if sucked down his ass by a vacuum. His asshole was smooth and easy to enter. I thought I was supposed to do this roughly, so I bounced Kelly's buns up and down on the mattress while he whimpered and blew his breath into my face.

Kelly strained into an even more abject position. He pushed his legs backwards farther and stuck his ass up higher. The toes, and then the soles of his sneakers were mashed upside down against the wall behind the bed. His knees were bent backwards so they touched the rumpled sheets, and his calves pressed meanly against his earlobes. We french-kissed while we fucked. I could smell cigarette smoke on his breath, and I tried to suck the tobacco flavor out of his tongue, as though I were sucking the last drops of fruit juice out of a Popsicle wrapper.

Kelly's ass was mushy and loose, too loose for me to hurt him. Maybe he had been fucked a hundred times already. More likely, his rear end had been distended by Moonshot Lewis, a black boy who lived on Kelly's corridor. Moonshot had jet black skin, skinny arms and legs that were too long, and a mastodon-sized cock (easily twice as big as mine) that swung in front of his body like a cinder block. His thin black body was shaped just like Kelly's. Moonshot could have satisfied Kelly's longing for rectal pain. While I fucked Kelly (more like vaginal intercourse than brute, gay ass-fucking), I imagined Moonshot grinding his way into Kelly's butt, their twin, gangly bodies double-helixed into hydraulic symbiosis, a squirming, animated yin-yang of black flesh and white boyhunger. The fantasy took me over the edge. My mind radiated when I came. I cupped my mouth over Kelly's nose and sucked salt-flavored mucus out of his nostrils. The cerebral mush of exploded brain bits dripped down the inner wall of my cranium. I lapsed into coma, and fell asleep down a bottomless shaft of unconsciousness. Kelly and I were hot, but Kelly and Moonshot were a fuck scene for the Hall of Fame.

I became very fond of Kelly, who liked me even though I was quiet. I unknowingly craved attention, and Kelly was one of the few people who paid any attention to me. He smiled like a sunbeam, laughed in his girlish voice, snapped my butt with his towel in the locker room after track practice. For a stretch of days, Kelly became moody and troubled. He wasn't winning in track ("falling short of his 'potential,'" said the coach). I stupidly thought Kelly was worried about the high jump and offered moronic suggestions to improve his performance. He smiled and shook his head in pity. "You're cool, Pete. Don't worry about it, okay?" I'd hoped Kelly would help me become friends with Cady Donaldson, or at least tell me more about him, but Kelly never wanted to talk about Cady.

※

My interest in Cady Donaldson never became sexual. It was more of an eerie, electrostatic obsession. His razor-sharp beauty cut through my psyche at light speed, penetrating into my subconscious. Did I love Cady more than T.J. because Cady looked more like a girl? The few times I tried to speak to him, a prickly static poured into my brain and my sight was blocked by yellow haze, like when you rise too quickly from a deep knee bend. I never understood why I reacted so oddly. The reason couldn't have been guilt over my queerness, because I was comfortable with my attraction to T.J. and Kelly. I wasn't afraid of gay sex, but was I afraid of gay love?

In his senior year, Cady changed his hairstyle from a conservative, preppy crop to the stringy, late-sixties "hippie" look, parted down the middle instead of on the side. I thought it ruined his beauty, diluted his aristocracy, and I hoped he would change back. Cady only went deeper into his Woodstock image. A few days before his graduation, he was caught smoking marijuana on campus (a capital offense under boarding school jurisprudence). I was in shock and terribly hurt, having internalized Briarwood's code of behavior lock, line, stock, hook, barrel, and sinker. I felt personally rejected by Cady's transgression.

The Headmaster decided not to expel Cady since it was so close to graduation and Cady had never been in trouble before. Cady was sent home for the last few days after final exams and returned for commencement. After the graduation ceremonies, I sat on the steps of Chase Hall and watched him load his suitcases into his father's Mercedes. I was terrified and near tears. I felt as though the last seconds of my life were ticking by. For an instant, Cady half smiled at me and his eyes sparkled meanly. He knew that I was suffering. Our nonverbal dialogue had been finite and precise: Cady knew I was in love with him. He just didn't care.

Later that day I rode the bus to New York for summer vacation. I leaned my head against the bus window and cried the whole way over a boy I'd barely ever spoken to.

7

☀ I can't say I was excited to be going home for summer. As I rode in the back of the Greyhound bus, headed for New York, I felt as if I were travelling in a spaceship to another planet. It didn't seem possible that a gas-powered vehicle could cover the spiritual distance between Briarwood and East Harlem. I leaned my head against the vibrating bus window. The blankness of the highway and the running tremor of the Greyhound put me in a meditative state. I closed my eyes and remembered the place where I grew up.

That place was the Jefferson Housing Projects, a collection of box-like buildings made from pale orange brick that sat on the eastern edge of Manhattan. This huge housing compound, lined and seamed with gray granite and metal fences, was a city within a city, doubly urban and thus doubly removed from the land of trees and moist, pungent earth I was travelling from. The street I lived on, East 112th, was a one-way strip of tarred-over cobble that bordered the projects to the south. It was often congested with traffic headed for the entrance ramp to the East River Drive. From my bedroom window I could always hear the sounds of car horns, the atomic-powered farts of accelerating engines, the screech of emergency stops. When I was ten, a boy my age was run over on this street by a tourist trying to get to the airport. Sitting in the back of the Greyhound, I thought of the speed bumps on the back roads of Old Greenwich, built to shear off the axle of a car going fast enough to kill a child.

Across 112th Street were dusty, eroded tenement houses, rows of them spanning the island from east to west, their fronts blackened over eons with soot, their wooden frames steeped with the smell of pesticide. My sister Joselyn and Russell lived in a tenement house, three blocks west of where we lived. I remembered the nights I'd climbed creaking stairs to baby-sit Joselyn's three children. One day the roach bomb brought every insect inside her walls panicking out into the open, hundreds of them crawling on the ceiling and the kitchen table, a crisis in the insect underworld like the great flood or the attack of the fifty-foot woman. My sister had stood in the middle of the kitchen, beating them off the walls with a broom.

My family had lived in East Harlem since I was two years old. My older brother Malcolm told me stories about our first apartment in a West Harlem tenement, but I had no memory of living anywhere but on East 112th Street.

Malcolm had also told me that our family was descended from African royalty. "We must be. Look at Mommy," he said, and I had nodded and agreed. I was terrifically proud and terrified of my mother. It seemed everyone was terrified of her.

Just two years before, I'd needed emergency surgery on my testicles. In the middle of the night my mother had taken me to the city hospital. When she returned to the hospital the morning after my operation, to find me recovering in the G.U. ward with ten very ill and elderly men — throat tubes, I.V.s, and wheezing, and bubbling spittle all around — she exploded in fury and demanded I be moved to a semiprivate room, which I was, within the hour.

She was the smartest woman in the projects, everyone knew, because she had two husbands who worked. My real father was a car factory foreman, and my unofficial stepfather Seth was a cook in a private hospital. Her woman friends in the projects were all extroverted and funny, like she was, and though she blended in with them — just one of the girls — she was tacitly recognized as the leader, the star of the show. Arguing with her was pointless; when she became angry — an at least daily occurrence — her face expanded to fill the room and her eyes swelled just as her facial features — brows, nose, lips — skewed towards a forceful, impaling center. In her fury she had always seemed to grow in size and power before my eyes.

East Harlem, or Spanish Harlem, is different from West Harlem. In Spanish Harlem, everywhere are the sounds of conga drums and horn music, the quick, tumbling rhythms and gum-smacking bite of the Spanish language. The Puerto Rican people lived separate lives from the blacks. Still, their culture filtered through into our world; they affected my life like a strong seasoning can affect a stew. Our next-door neighbors, the Rojas, were Puerto Rican, and we almost never spoke to them. I sometimes caught a glimpse of their living room through their open door as one of the Rojas was coming or going. I often wondered about the different world in their apartment — did their mother hit their father like my mother sometimes did? Did the brothers fight over who had to do the dishes? Sometimes I could hear the Spanish-language television station from outside their door.

The landscape along the Greyhound's route was becoming incrementally more urban. I was becoming more anxious. I wasn't sure if I was fit for Harlem anymore. I felt so comfortable now in my sports jackets and cuffed slacks, and if I listened to myself I could hear how my speech had become proper and lilting. I wasn't a tough kid anymore, not that I ever really had been, but the code of ghetto manhood had once made sense to me. Now I was sure it did not. What if somebody started a fight with me? Did I still know how to fight? Would my preppy accent make me a likely target?

I'd had two fights in my entire life. The first was a mild and brief affair with a boy I liked named Wilbur. We shoved and cursed each other for about five minutes. I don't remember what the fight was about, and I don't think we ever actually hit each other.

My second fight was with a Puerto Rican boy named Skito. I didn't know Skito and had nothing to do with him, but Skito's little brother Willie had started trouble in the sandpile with my little brother Ken. Willie was older than Ken, and I was older than Willie, but Skito and I were the same age; by the traditions of interfamily warfare in the projects, Skito and I were obliged to defend our kid brothers.

Getting into a fight was like jumping off a high diving board. You were instantly committed, there was no turning back, and now you didn't know what was going to happen. You'd relinquished your fate to the momentum of pride and the will of the crowd of spectators that always gathered around and screamed for action. Usually, there wasn't much. Most fights were more like dances, two boys circling in esoteric boxing stances and strange circular gestures with the fists. I think the idea was the stranger your stance and the more schizoid your hand gestures, the more terror you struck into your opponent. I always thought this was silly. If you're going to fight, fight. If you're going to run, run. But don't dance around like an autistic scarecrow. I didn't box, I wrestled, because I watched professional wrestling on TV, and because boxing took skill and I didn't think I had any, and because I was too embarrassed to strike a funny boxing stance.

Skito started circling me and winding up his fist, expecting me to do the same. I dived headfirst into his stomach, wrestled him to the ground, and climbed on his back. In seconds he was helpless. I pounded on his back and yanked his hair. I could have banged his forehead into the ground and knocked him out, but I wasn't mean enough. Skito's big brother grabbed me from behind and pulled me off of him.

Skito jumped up raging. His nose was spilling blood where I'd scraped it on the concrete. He punched me hard in the stomach and I fell backwards into the crowd. Then my brother Malcolm stepped in and stopped the fight. Skito's friends led him away, and a little black boy congratulated me for winning. "You fight good," he said, and I think he meant that I skipped the dancing and got right to the action.

Skito's brother asked me later if I wanted to fight Skito again. "You think you bad 'cause you fought Skito," he said. I wasn't interested. That punch in the stomach had really hurt.

One of the worst feelings I ever had growing up was seeing my brother Malcolm beaten in a fight. I was coming back from the supermarket, and I saw a crowd of boys hollering. Through the crowd I recognized Malcolm's sneakers and shorts sticking out on the ground. Malcolm was on his back and another boy was on top of him. It didn't matter that the boy was a year older than Malcolm, or that he came from the Johnson Houses, four blocks west of Jefferson, which was like coming from another province. Malcolm's defeat made me feel vulnerable, as though a gap had been torn in my family line of defense.

✺

I arrived at the Port Authority Bus Terminal with my suitcase and duffel bag and took the subway uptown to 116th Street. Then I walked south and east to our apartment building. My mother saw me coming and called to me from our fifth-story window.

"Didn't Malcolm meet you at the station?" she asked when I got upstairs.

"No," I said.

"I told him to meet you at the station. Did you have trouble with your bags?"

"No," I repeated. I lumbered to my bedroom with my duffel bag bouncing against my knee.

I had a feeling of vague oppression as I entered the room I'd shared with Malcolm growing up. I looked at the walls, which were bare except for a small, square painting of a farm house. In my room at school I'd hung up posters of pro football stars and the TV threesome of amazon commandoes. I tapped on the cage of our parakeet Pip, and wondered if my face still meant anything to him. I dropped my bags and then stopped in to look around my younger brothers' room. Ken and Tyrone had both left already for Boys' Club summer camp. Our beagle puppy Caesar stayed in their room. He was ecstatic to see me, jiggling like a slinky and fretting with happiness. I sat down on Tyrone's bed and played with Caesar until it was time for dinner.

My stepfather was working late, so my mother and I had dinner alone. She had made cheeseburgers and french fries and baked a cream pie. Sometimes when we were alone together, my mother entertained me like a stand-up comic. I always suspected she was showing off, since I could never keep up with her sparkling charisma. My own puddle of emotions, no more than a finger's depth, was pitiable next to her Croton Reservoir of energy and feeling. In her best moods, she was like a circus bareback rider on a champion horse, or a surfer at one with a monstrous wave, or a chameleon-like wizard, metamorphosing himself with repeated taps on the head from his magic wand. At times I felt my mind was moving in slow motion, trudging through quicksand, while hers darted around like an annoying sprite.

Tonight she was in a comic mood. What a day she'd had. There was the nitwit at the deli counter who tried to sell her a bruised tomato, and the idiot bank teller who shortchanged her twenty dollars. She made him recount the money three times until he realized she was right. And when an overweight businessman behind her in the line had complained that she was taking too long, she had "blasted him to kingdom come." "He'll think twice before he opens *his* mouth again, that fish-faced flunky." There was a glint in her eye as she said this. I could just see her disrupting the entire bank, demanding to see the manager. By now I was sure she'd earned among the bank staff the proud appellation "that *woman*," just as she had in the supermarket and the housing office and on at least three floors in our apartment building.

This was how I'd remembered her since childhood. Taxi drivers who tried to pad the route, delinquent janitors, slow-moving bank tellers, and rude department store cashiers were regularly and excessively rebuked. She raised electrical storms like a thunder goddess. She was an avenging angel against incompetence, the wielder of a cosmic fury we could only pray was guided by reason and justice.

※

That night from my bedroom window I listened to conga drums, honking horns, and voices in the street. A cherry bomb exploded. I could hear the Rojas children arguing in Spanish through the window next door. The city sounds formed a living voice, sprays and bursts of sound, formless and disordered yet somehow of a whole, like a postmodern orchestral piece. I was reminded that my neighborhood was a "dangerous" place. I let my imagination run until I was exhilarated with fear. I peered out into the darkness, half expecting some fluid, formless evil to lunge through the window and spirit me away.

A police siren started in the distance, crescendoed, and then faded towards the north. That's the Doppler effect, I thought, remembering my earth science lecture on sound waves. I wondered what the officers in that police car were thinking, what horror had triggered their emergency. A shiver of relief ran through me. It felt safe to be indoors. I felt cold and warm at once, just as if I'd chanced upon a wooden shack in the forest in the middle of a rainstorm, thick drops splattering through the doorway, bouncing up into my face, and enough damp chill in the air to make me cherish my protection. I'd known this tingling sensation often as a child, I'd felt it sitting on this same windowsill, but I'd forgotten it in Connecticut. The absence of threat had rendered my emotions bland.

I undressed and got under my covers. I was too agitated with fantasies of danger to sleep. My pores were still open and my skin still tingled. Out of bedtime habit, I started to think about boys.

I thought first of Cady Donaldson. I tried to stir up some of the misery I was feeling earlier, but it seemed I had already forgotten I loved him. Cady was gone forever, I knew, and I'd cried most of the hurt out of my system on the bus ride home. I thought instead of T.J. His mother had driven up to school to pick him up, and I'd said hello to her and good-bye to him for the summer, just that morning, though it seemed like weeks ago. I wondered what T.J. was doing right then at home. He played a lot of tennis in the summer, he'd told me. I could see him now in his white shorts and low-top sneakers, cotton socks drooping over his ankles, tossing his head to flick the hair out of his eyes. Another flush ran through my body as I remembered what he had done to me only days before.

Just then a thought hit me. There were boys in New York, too! All the Puerto Rican boys in the Boys' Club and at the swimming pool. All my old friends from summer day camp. I was queer now, and maybe one or two of them were, too. The next day I would start looking for my summer boyfriend. The prospect was relaxing. For the first time I was glad to be home. I rolled over and went to sleep.

※

I awoke uneasily the next morning, lingering in semi-sleep for several minutes. I heard a bird singing outside my window, and for an instant I thought I was back at school. Then I remembered the tall oak tree in the grass lot in front of our building, and the sparrows that had always nested right outside our window. I sat up on the edge of my bed.

On all my vacations, I never felt I was really back home until I had awakened in my own bed. Starting an entire day in New York made it official. I stood up and looked out the window. Two boys were playing marbles in the parking lot, and a class of preschoolers, lined up in pairs, was following its leader up 112th Street. In the distance they looked like the tail of a caterpillar. I'd slept late, it was about ten o'clock. I got dressed and went into the kitchen.

My mother was slicing carrots at the kitchen table. She said good morning, and then sent me across the street to buy a quart of milk and a half dozen eggs. She had always sent me across the street to buy milk and eggs, since I was seven, and I was annoyed to return to a forgotten routine. I felt no sentiment for any of these childhood reminders: sparrows and conga drums and milk and eggs. No one ever sent me to the store at prep school, I grumbled to myself as I crossed 112th Street.

The store across the street was run by three Italian brothers, the Izetta brothers, and an old Italian woman named Maggie. A short, black-haired Puerto Rican boy named Hector had worked for the Izetta brothers for years. I had always liked Hector. I liked his ashy, golden skin, his translucent mustache, and the way he deepened his voice to sound tough. I looked right at him when I went into the store this time, hoping he would notice that I'd been away, but he ignored me. He was talking with the old woman Maggie in his cute, tough voice. Hector had made his girlfriend pregnant and he wanted to marry her. "Marry her," said Maggie. "You gotta marry her, Hector." The oldest brother, Joey Izetta, kept telling Hector he was stupid. "They're giving away free milk, and this dummy wants to buy a cow."

I bought my milk and eggs and left, displeased that Hector was getting married. He was only sixteen years old!

"Shit!" I said aloud as I rode alone in the elevator back up to our apartment.

I went into the kitchen and put the eggs in the refrigerator. I put the milk on the table. My mother was chopping celery on the breadboard. With each slice, she made a hard knock on the board with the knife handle. "I'm making barbecued meat loaf," she said. I poured myself a bowl of Corn Pops and sat down.

"Where's Malcolm?" I asked.

"I don't know where Malcolm is."

"How's he doing?"

"The same."

"He dropped out of the program?"

"No, he didn't drop out of the program." She put the knife down on the breadboard. "He got *kicked* out of the program." Her eyes turned glassy with anger. Her voice seemed to echo off the kitchen walls. "He *told* me he finished the program, but I didn't believe him. So I called over there. He tested positive for marijuana *and* heroin. Marijuana *and* heroin."

I turned back to my Corn Pops, cowed by her outburst. My mother was still glaring at me. I turned and looked out the window. Two young girls were playing on a tricycle in the parking lot and screaming at each other. I looked as far as I could to the west, but the cityscape of the Johnson Houses blocked my view of the horizon. My mother calmed down and started chopping again.

"How's that fella at your school doing?"

I played dumb, I knew who she meant. "What fella?"

"You know what fella I'm talking about. I met him that first night. In Mr. Bennett's house."

"T.J.?" I smiled to myself as I scooped the last spoonful of cereal into my mouth. She asked about T.J. every time I came home.

"That's right. I knew it was T.J. or T.B. or P.J., or something."

I turned to her with a wide smile on my face. I almost felt like laughing. "He's doing fine." I got up and put my cereal bowl in the sink and went out of the kitchen.

※

My brother Malcolm was a junkie. Not a totally wasted, garbage-pail junkie, like you might see in a crime movie. He didn't slur his words or wear ragged clothes. No, Malcolm dressed. Lizard-skin shoes; rabbit-fur hats; leather, suede, or cashmere coats. Fancy colored slacks, orange or yellow or bright red. We figured he either stole the clothes or stole to get the money to buy them. Malcolm was twenty years old, and he'd only recently become a dope addict. He'd volunteered for the army at seventeen. He'd even volunteered to go to Vietnam because he wanted to kill, but they wouldn't send him because my brother Basil was already in 'Nam. Malcolm went AWOL from the army after a year and came back home a heroin addict. A fresh, fast, hunky, young dope addict.

Malcolm always knew he would end up a junkie. He told me so when he was fourteen. He came home one night, drunk on Bacardi Rum, and stumbled into the bottom bunk bed. "I'm afraid I'm going to be a junkie when I grow up," he told me. This was an amazing thing for a fourteen-year-old to say, a statement packed with moral and metaphysical complexities of knowledge and intent and fate and blame. But when Malcolm came home on his first furlough in the army, he'd been transformed into something stupid. He wasn't afraid of drugs anymore. "Only people with weak minds become addicted," he lectured me then. "My mind is strong enough to handle it."

I was terrified by drugs, because my oldest brother Jackson had died of an overdose when I was twelve.

We held a memorial service at the drug rehabilitation center. Jackson's dope addict friends from the rehab program spoke at the service. The dope addicts said wonderful things about Jackson. I believed them. My brother was a good person.

At least he'd made an effort to support his children. Before Jackson's wife left him, he did a fair job of fathering his boy and girl. Without his kids, he couldn't hold his grip and fell back into heroin. I thought of the night his first boy David was born, the aura around Jackson, the light in his eyes. I thought of that the night he died.

My mother cried wretchedly at the memorial service. Horrid, guttural noises, the worst sounds I've ever heard; harsh, choking sounds, as if her throat were coated with rust. At one point she started rocking forward. I thought she was having a heart attack. My brothers and I got up and circled close around her. I thought she was going to die right in front of me. She just kept choking and crying. Her eyes were wild and unfixed and filled with tears. It was as though she couldn't see us, didn't know we were there.

For months after Jackson died I lived in fear. I felt inside of me a need to scream, except there wasn't anything there to scream at. There was another boy in a room somewhere, I thought, and he was the one screaming. The room he was in had white walls and was empty, and he was sitting on a chair. I didn't know where he was, but I knew what he felt. I was connected to him by ESP. I knew how he was feeling, and that was what I was feeling inside, except I didn't scream, because it wouldn't do any good. I was here, I wasn't in that room, and I couldn't see what it was that was making him scream.

※

That afternoon I ran two miles around the track in Jefferson Park. It was my fancy to pretend I was a horse, and I galloped around the curves, springing forward out of my shanks, pridefully lifting my knees. During the winter film festival at school, we'd seen a film called *The Loneliness of* the Long Distance Runner, about an English barstol runner who obstinately stopped yards short of winning a race trophy to spite his prison warden. The title of the film was my chosen mantra; I chanted it in rhythm as I ran, filling my mind with it, gaining strength. The chant had propelled me through the fields at school on misty mornings. It became the theme song for long stretches of my life, like the one that was just beginning this summer.

I exhausted myself in the last quarter mile of my run, then lay on my back in the grass to catch my breath. The clouds overhead were caught in a quick wind travelling north. I followed one puffy nimbus mound as far as I could with my eyes, wishing I could hitch a ride on its polar-bound journey. I felt vaguely troubled as I lost myself in the eternally rising blue. There were faint tremors just below my skin, and an uneasiness in my stomach as though I'd eaten poorly. I lost track of the time. I might have lain there for an hour. A dog barking nearby brought my thoughts back from the sky. I turned my head sideways on the ground and, through a jungle of grass blades, saw a long-haired setter nipping playfully at his master's pant leg. Hard pebbles were pressing into my back. A caterpillar was crawling on my leg near my knee. I flicked off the bug with my finger and stretched my arm around back to brush off the dirt and stones. Then I picked up my towel and bathing suit from where I'd hidden them under a bush, and walked towards the park swimming pool.

The pool was free of charge in the morning, but I knew there would be more boys in the afternoon. I avoided the cashier's eyes as I paid my fifty cents and pushed through the turnstile. I felt sneaky and smart, as though I were walking into the movies with a phony ticket. I walked towards the boys' dressing hall. I could already hear water splashing and run-amok screams, the orchestral mesh of squeals, yelps, and hollers of children already in the pool. "Which one will it be?" I wondered.

The dressing hall was a large, square room, empty except for a row of foot-high benches nailed to the floor. The cement floor was damp everywhere, and in some spots there were puddles of water. The scent of chlorine had soaked into the floor and walls. A single low-wattage bulb hanging from the ceiling cast the hall in what seemed like brown light. On one side of the room was the clothes check window. The attendant there was a handsome, stocky young man with an auburn crew cut, wearing a green park uniform. I stripped out of my track shorts and shoes and stuffed them into one of the numbered wire baskets stacked by the clothes check window. The attendant took my basket and handed me an elastic band with my basket number on it.

When I was in summer day camp, years before I went to Briarwood, I came to this pool almost every day. The chlorine smell in the hall and this clothes-checking routine brought back memories of these earlier summers, when the sex in me had been just a formless cloud. Ronnie James had reached out and grabbed my dick in this hall. I still remembered Wilbur, the golden-skinned black boy who took his time drying his loose-hanging, golden brown dick, three shades darker than the rest of his body. And Willie, the tiny dark-skinned boy who had jumped out of the toilet stall with his pants still down around his ankles and his arms up in the air, scaring me half to death. And Guy, who could have been my twin, the boy I'd fallen in love with, except I didn't know it at the time. I always gave Guy my cookies and soda at lunch. I also started a fight with a Puerto Rican kid who tried to take my place as Guy's lineup partner; I must have been in love to be so violent.

I didn't think of approaching any black boys now. It didn't make sense, somehow, that any of them would be queer. Besides, they all knew me and my family. Their mothers knew my mother. I hardly knew any of the Puerto Rican boys. I knew some of their faces, but almost none of their names, except Skito and his little brother Willie. They lived in their own little Puerto Rican world, stayed with their friends and their brothers and sisters, and that distance made me feel safe. At least one of them is going to like me, I thought.

I put on my bathing suit and looked around the dressing hall. Two thin, brown boys were at the far end near the entrance to the pool. One was standing and rubbing his back with his towel. The other was stretched out on the bench, his feet pointed apart and his arms folded behind his head. Water was dripping from their hair and bathing suits onto the floor. They were both about thirteen years old. I looked over at them, but they were talking and giggling and paid me no attention.

I went outside and dived into the swimming pool. Most of the kids in the pool were younger than me, some very young. I swam around and tried to make contact, but everyone was splashing up too much water and having too much fun and making too much noise. I got out and walked over to the stone benches by the gate, where you could look out at the spectators in the park. Two handsome boys were lying on their towels sunning themselves. The elastic bands with their basket numbers were wrapped around their ankles, and their eyes were closed, though I knew they weren't asleep. I sat down on the bench by the gate, and looked at them but they didn't budge. The bench was made of concrete and was scraping against the bottom of my thigh. I thought to myself that those concrete benches were stupid and useless, since everyone in the pool had on bathing suits and the concrete would scrape everyone's skin. I kept waiting for the two boys to stop pretending they were asleep, but they just twitched their feet and turned their heads away from me, nestling back into their folded forearms.

I got up and walked to the ten-foot diving pool. Some older boys, about nineteen or twenty, were jumping from the high board. They were muscular, but none of them looked especially cute. They looked more like men than boys. I dived into the pool from the side and swam to the bottom, and then back up again. I did this over and over several times, then swam to the edge of the pool and propped myself up on my elbows. I peered back at the wading pool and looked for some cute boy who was watching me, but my eyes were stinging and I could barely see. "Shit!" I said to myself and pulled myself up out of the water. I went into the dressing hall and got my clothes basket, got dressed, and went home.

8

☀ The two detectives knocked on our door Sunday morning. I looked through the peephole and then stepped back from the door quietly. The detectives knocked again.

"Who's at the door?" my mother called from her bedroom.

I went to her door. "Two men in suits. I don't recognize them." She opened the door and gave me a doubtful, almost bemused look. Then she brushed past me and went to the front door.

"Can I help you?" she said through the peephole.

"We're the police. We'd like to talk to you, please."

She opened the door and the detectives showed their badges. They were two heavy black men, one with a beard, both with bellies that stretched the buttons on their white shirts.

"Are you Malcolm Givens's mother?"

"Yes."

"We're looking for Malcolm Givens."

My mother stepped back and let the officers in.

"There's been a serious crime. We would rather not mention any details right now. We just want to talk to Malcolm. If he didn't do it, then that gives us a good idea who *did* do it, and that's what we want to know. We just want to rule your son out."

"Well, I haven't seen him."

"When did you last see him?"

"A week ago. He doesn't live here, you know."

※

Malcolm had a criminal record. He'd already spent six months on Riker's Island for stealing a leather coat from Bloomingdale's — and injuring a security guard. He'd walked through the electric eye, triggered the alarm, then punched the guard in the head and ran. He sold the coat to his friend Manny. When Manny was stopped by the police, they recognized the doctoring done on stolen coats. Malcolm had torn out the security attachment and sewn up the inseam. Manny told the police who sold him the coat. They arrested Malcolm for assault and robbery, and since there were video pictures of the theft, his defense attorney advised him to plead guilty. This happened when he was sixteen.

Then there were the watches. Malcolm came out of the army a heroin addict. He needed money for drugs, and he figured he could sell the watches to get it. He hid in a department store changing room by removing the insulation panels in the ceiling and climbing up into a ventilation shaft. Apparently, he planned to hide a rack of watches in the garbage can and return the next morning to retrieve them. That way he could break a window to get out of the store that night, and if he was caught he wouldn't have any goods on him. He was surprised in the bathroom by the night watchman, who clubbed him with a flashlight, wrestled him to the floor, and cuffed him. The scar on his forehead is permanent. He served another six months for burglary.

※

The detectives left and didn't come back, so I assumed they found the person who did whatever it was they didn't want to mention. What I felt when they left was a mixture: an exaggerated sense of threat, and an absurd sense of being offended — how dare they? My mother thought I was silly, reacting as if the detectives were muggers or axe-murderers, but what she didn't see was my bewilderment that the police were actually there, in our house. I was shell-shocked by the actuality of their presence, as if someone had hit me in the head with a pan.

That night gunshots were fired in the parking lot downstairs below my window.

✺

Malcolm showed up at our apartment the following Friday afternoon. My mother and stepfather were out at work, and I was home alone. He had a woman with him.

His eyes darted aside as soon as I opened the door. "Peter!" he said.

"Hi, Malcolm."

"Lisa, this is my brother Peter."

"Hello, Peter," Lisa said.

They came in and sat on the living room sofa. Malcolm was wearing a new blue windbreaker with black silk pants and black dress shoes. Lisa was in blue jeans, white toeless heels, and a man's white shirt, with the sleeves rolled up over her elbows and the front tied in a knot over her navel.

"Wait a minute," Malcolm said. He went into the kitchen and came back with two glasses of soda. He set them on the coffee table and sat down with his arm around Lisa's shoulder.

"So how is school?" he asked.

"Fine," I said. "I'm trying out for varsity football in the fall. I think I'm going to make it."

"You number one yet?"

"No, still number two."

"Lisa," Malcolm said, leaning forward. He was speaking in a hushed, submissive voice. "My brother goes to private school in Connecticut. He's doing really well, he's like number two in his class. And then, medical school, right?" He gestured towards me with his hand.

"Probably law school," I said.

"Oh, that's nice," Lisa said flatly, curling towards Malcolm. She tugged on the zipper of Malcolm's windbreaker and smiled. "So what's cooking, sugar?"

"Peter, we're going to hang out in the back for a while, okay?"

"Okay," I said.

"Are you minding the house? You can go out for a while. I'm going to be here at least an hour."

"Okay."

I went outside and across the street to the Izetta Brothers delicatessen. Hector and Maggie were there alone. I walked to the freezer and got a pineapple sherbert, then walked up to the counter. Hector took my money and rang up the sale.

"Since when you been working the register?" I asked.

"They always let me work the register," he said indignantly. I stiffened and turned to walk out, smitten by the meanness in Hector's voice. He doesn't know I love him, I thought. I walked across 112th Street and went back upstairs.

When I got back to my apartment, there was a pungent smell coming from the back bedroom, Ken and Tyrone's room. The smell was thick and sweet, and could have come from burning almonds or plastic. I walked to the back of the hallway, but the door was closed. I listened but didn't hear anything, so I went back and sat in the living room. I turned on the radio and took out a magazine and sat down to read.

After a half hour, my mother called from work. I told her Malcolm was home, and she asked to speak to him.

"He's in the back," I said.

"Go get him!" she hollered.

I walked back and knocked on the door of the back bedroom. This time I could hear voices inside.

"What is it?" Malcolm called through the door.

"Go away," said Lisa, laughing.

"Mommy wants to talk to you."

Malcolm opened the door. He was sitting against the wall naked, a towel in his lap, reaching up from the floor with his hand on the knob. Lisa was naked too, with a rubber tube around her arm and a syringe in her left hand. She sat on the floor glaring at me.

"What did you say?" said Malcolm.

"Mommy's on the phone. She wants to talk to you."

"Damn, why did you tell her I was here?" he said, stumbling as he stood up. He wrapped Lisa's shirt around his waist and slipped his feet into my brother Ken's bedroom slippers.

I followed him into the living room. He picked up the phone and started muttering into the receiver. He was facing me, with his head lifted backwards and a pained, confused look in his eyes. He raised his voice for a second, and then he was silent. He kept drawing his breath as if he were trying to get a word in.

I went back to the bedroom. Lisa was still naked, sitting up on a pillow with her knees together. The rubber tube was lying on the floor in front of her. I stared at her in silence and she stared back. We stood like that for several moments. Then she leaned forward and flicked the door closed with her fingertips.

I heard the phone slam from the living room. Malcolm came back through the hallway.

"Don't ever tell her I'm here, you hear me?"

"You shouldn't be doing that stuff here," I said.

"Doing what stuff?"

"Heroin."

"That's not heroin," he said and pushed past me. He went into the room and closed the door behind him. About ten minutes later, he and Lisa came out fully dressed and left the apartment. Malcolm didn't say anything, he just let the front door slam behind him.

It wasn't hatred I felt towards Malcolm at that moment. What I felt was a lost emotion, something more diffuse than hate — a question for me to dwell on, a thought hiding in the shadows. There were flickers of pain beneath my eyelids, causing me to squint. I was no more than blandly agitated.

If I didn't hate Malcolm, it was because I was afraid to. I knew it would show, and then he would hurt me. I feared Malcolm because violence was in his nature and not in mine. I didn't feel like a coward, though. I knew Malcolm was fated to spend time in prison. His drug habits, too, would surely lead him hand in hand to hell. Strangely, I thought his pushing us around and getting away with it now was his due — advance compensation for the terrible price he'd pay in the future. His terrible future would redeem my cowardice, I believed, and this belief allowed me to stand by grim and mute while Malcolm polluted my mother's home, without despising my own weakness. This was a rationalization, of course, and it worked, but only so well. There had to be a fury hidden somewhere within me, somewhere inside a stifled wish to fight.

If I hated Malcolm at all, it was not because he stole from my mother and shot dope. It was because he dared me to stop him and I couldn't. He shoved my cowardice down my throat.

※

It seemed very still in Harlem that summer. Everything seemed to be happening at a distance, the voices of kids playing were like echoes in a canyon. Most of my friends from public school or summer day camp had discovered girls, and I felt I was intruding on their sex life if I talked to them. Everyone was a stranger to me.

Every day I did my running and training so I'd be ready to play football when I returned to school in the fall. I ran from my house through Jefferson Park, then along the East River Drive to the cabled drawbridge that crossed the East

River to Ward's Island. Sometimes I'd spend the entire day on Ward's Island. There were picnic areas and ball fields there, and a private rest home for war veterans. At the center of the island were rough hilly terrain and uncut forest. The center was unapproachable, and I knew nothing about it.

Further into the island stood two massive pillars of the Triboro Bridge. They swelled up in the distance from behind the thorny mound at the island's center, inching fully into view as I rounded the island's curve until they loomed monstrously before me. On sunny days, the Triboro cast its shadow across a flat field of grass. I slowed to a trot, then meekly ventured into the shade. It was always cooler under the bridge. The grass there was wet, and the earth soggy and aromatic. I looked up at the black iron underside of the highway. The rumble of cars and trucks overhead made loud, angry echoes against the gigantic granite pillars. The echoes became louder — more frightening — when I looked overhead. Still I couldn't resist the urge to glance upwards and scare myself mortally. I stood beneath the mass of rattling iron and orange granite, and terror rushed to fill me, spreading in an instant from my head out to my fingertips. I was afraid that the bridge might collapse. Could I run clear of the falling steel plates in time? I felt compelled to fall to my knees, even to prostrate myself on the grass. I could only bear to be under that bridge for a few moments; I stepped back out onto the sunlit grass and sun-dried dirt and shook the fear out of my bones.

It was good to run along the edge of the island, near the water, since the picnickers kept their children away from the bank. The water lapped up against the rocks on the island's shore, and a faint stink of pollution floated inland when the river tide was high. One day I saw a water rat, as big as a watermelon, disappear between two gray wet rocks. The East River was the dirtiest river in New York. All the kids in my neighborhood knew this because our mothers warned us not to swim or fish in the river.

My stride was getting stronger every day. To my surprise I could easily run halfway round the island, to the Triboro and then back to the East River Drive. From there I had to stop running and walk about a mile home. All the way I walked, I daydreamed about boys.

※

Keith Hanson called me up at home one day. He was coming into the city, and he asked me if I wanted to see a movie. We went to see the new science fiction feature and then went to the penny arcade in Times Square. Then we stopped off for hot dogs at Nedick's. We talked about our summer jobs. Keith was working at his dad's electronics shop on Long Island. I was working on a neighborhood newspaper at the East Harlem community center, typing and writing articles and drawing cartoons. Keith told me he didn't want to go back to Briarwood, but his mother wouldn't let him quit.

I didn't say anything when he told me that. I couldn't wait to get back to school. I was festering inside, I was sick of hot, white concrete and loud, screaming, running children and boys with their arms around girls' shoulders (what *were* they whispering in those ears?). None of the cute Puerto Ricans were paying any attention to me.

Keith and I made a date to go to Jones Beach on the weekend. I left him at the Long Island Railroad terminal and took the subway back home.

※

When I got home my mother was seated on the sofa. She seemed not to notice that I'd come in. I walked over to the sofa, and she turned abruptly to look at me. Her eyes were glaring, her pupils were small and focused on the bridge of her nose. She had an envelope in her hand.

"What's wrong?" I asked.

"They arrested your brother — again."

"For what?"

"I got a call this morning, and this was in the mail." She handed me the envelope. "He wants me to post bail."

In the envelope was a handwritten letter from Malcolm and a copy of a criminal complaint. Possession and sale of narcotics, possession of a firearm, resisting arrest, and assault on a police officer. And a bail notice of $750.

"You can't pay this. He'll skip bail."

She didn't answer me. She kept turning and pausing and looking at different places in the room.

"All you would be doing is wasting the money. And if he skips bail and they catch him, he'll get even more time."

"No he won't," she said nastily. "Read the letter, smarty. He could be waiting a year just for a hearing."

I stopped and read the letter from beginning to end. Malcolm denied doing anything. "I was minding my business on the street," he'd written. "The pig challenged my black manhood and I refused to bow and scrape like a nigger and an Uncle Tom. So he arrested me and planted drugs. That is the way of the pig."

"And he says the jail guards might hurt him because he's accused of hitting a cop," she said.

"That's what he gets for being a junkie."

My mother stood up and looked out the living room window. "I'm going to pay his bail," she said.

"You can't do this! You've got to be rational. I know he's your son, but — can't you see? — paying his bail is just a mistake. It's not a hope. It's just a mistake."

She was still looking out the window. She turned and sat back down on the sofa. "Don't you think I know that?" she said wearily, angrily.

"I don't believe it—"

"Shut up, Peter. I'm not leaving him in jail. Do you understand? You can come with me or you can stay here, but I'm not letting those bastards—" she hissed, "—those *bastards* have him."

※

I went with her a week later down to the House of Detention on 13th Street near the West Side highway, in a no-man's neighborhood I couldn't recognize as part of New York. I didn't know then that the streets around this city jailhouse teemed with gay men at night, or that ten years later I would haunt these same streets like a vampire, cruising for sex at insanely late hours.

We went to the desk and paid a fat, hairy black man by check. My mother signed some papers and the man told us to wait. I looked around the lobby. The floors and walls were smeared with dirt. An air vent was covered with a puffy layer of black dust, thick as sponge. Black scuff marks had worn through much of the gray spotted linoleum. Pairs of police officers were leading men back and forth in ankle chains and handcuffs. Again I'm ashamed to admit this, but what good is it to you, my reader, if I don't tell the truth? I was infuriated. Why was I, a Briarwood schoolboy, standing here in the House of Detention? You may think me an ass for saying that, but it is honestly how I felt.

Malcolm came out through a heavy iron door and hugged my mother. Then he reached for my hand and shook it. He was speaking clearly and smiling. His demeanor was officious, celebratory, as if he'd just been married or graduated from college and expected congratulations. I realized he was trying to cast his release from jail as a joyous rather than shameful occasion. He told my mother he loved her. He looked at me again, now with frozen eyes, hesitated, then spoke. "Thanks for coming, brother," he said, again smiling. The falseness of this show was palpable. It was horrid and eerie, to know that he hated me though he hid it so well. It was as if Malcolm's spirit, possessed of shame and hate, had left his body and was floating around that dingy hallway, spewing silent and invisible malevolence, while his body smiled and postured and talked with clarity and utter falseness.

He stayed at home for a couple of days. He sat around eating bacon and eggs in his bare feet and stayed up late watching television. I was afraid to show my contempt for him, and so when he asked me to play a game of chess, I obliged. He beat me several times. Then we played poker and he won again. We discussed politics and he matched me thought for thought. But I'd always known that Malcolm was smarter than I was.

After two days he disappeared. He took my mother's camera and my stepfather's gold watch and my checkbook from the Green River National Bank. I wasn't worried since there was only five dollars in my account. A week later I got a call from the baseball stadium ticket office. Malcolm had paid for fifty dollars' worth of baseball tickets with one of my checks. I asked the man calling if he ever wondered what a drug addict in New York was doing with a bank account in Green River, Connecticut. Malcolm's impression of me had apparently been flawless, down to my newly formed Connecticut accent; he had convinced the ticket clerk he went to private school. (Malcolm had been studying my preppy style at home. Once he asked me to talk to him using "big words," and now I knew why.) I thought I was obliged to pay the check, but my mother picked up the phone and told the man he was out of luck.

In six weeks the bail bondsman foreclosed on the bail deposit. We didn't see Malcolm again all summer. In September, I returned to Briarwood.

Part 3

9

The Thayers had always sent their sons to Briarwood. Their name could be found on athletic plaques and school trophies dating back a hundred years. After an American president and an infamous literary laureate, they were Briarwood's most illustrious alumni. They controlled the private banking house of Bechton & Thayer. Their scientific foundation was world famous, and there had been several prominent appointments from the family to the foreign service.

In my junior year, Christopher Thayer came to Briarwood. I already knew Ethan Thayer, Christopher's older brother, from the senior class. Ethan was captain of the hockey team and a tennis star and vice president of the student council. I'd always had a crush on Ethan — more social than erotic. He was tough and sporty (though slight of build), oaken blond and occasionally prim. He played guitar, like I did, and I'd sat with him many mornings at breakfast and talked about music, or sometimes about baseball. Ethan was one of my favorite people, so I was naturally excited to learn, on my first day back from summer, that his kid brother Chris would be coming to our school.

There was a rumor running about school, that first day, that the second Thayer heir had been expelled from Whitehaven Academy for an unknown but reputedly heinous reason. The rumor added spice to my curiosity.

※

I was happy to be back at school. Though the shocks of the previous summer were past, my soul still resonated with fear and resentment. As I stood on Governor's Hill, removed from the urban ghetto, I felt more than ever that I had returned to an enchanted forest, a world of unreality. And I was relieved.

Briarwood was most beautiful in autumn. Autumn is the most sensuous season, I believe, the most rarefied and vivid. People associate the spring with rebirth, but for me that attribute has always best described the autumn, the time to return to school. Briarwood had begun to determine my life cycle. There was the traditional fine blend of colors — reds and browns and yellows — so potent in its ability to infuse my mind with new hope. There was also that fresh, New England snap of cold in the air. This is what I loved, what I'd missed. My lungs drank in the cool air hungrily, like a long deprived connoisseur.

For straight boys, the first days of school were drudgery. If I tried hard, I could sense their regret at the summer's passing, their reluctant adjustment to the new school year. But imagine me, my queerness in full bloom, back among this abundance of t-shirted adolescents. I was teeming with eagerness. I could not have been happier.

I strolled around the campus and watched all the first-day-back activity. There was the usual bustle of moving into dorms — roommates helping each other with trunks, stereo speakers hefted onto shoulders, spindly new boys dragging duffel bags up flights of stairs. There were administrative duties also, such as registering for classes and checking in with Dean Press. After moving all my belongings into my room, I went over to Chase Hall to take care of these errands.

Out of curiosity, I looked at the posted list of room assignments and was thrilled to discover that Christopher Thayer had been assigned to room with T.J. Adams in the Milburger Dormitory. I was already eager to see T.J. to find out about his summer and to tell him about mine. Now I had to talk to him at once. I ran out of Chase Hall, across the quad, and up the stairs of Milburger.

I burst into T.J.'s room without knocking. A boy was there alone, looking out an open window, his hands tucked under the flaps of a blue wool blazer into the pockets of white corduroy trousers. This was Christopher, I assumed. He was blonder than his brother and a bit more fully built. His amber eyes shone in natural affinity with the autumn sun. He turned towards me, startled, and took his hands out of his pockets.

"You must be looking for Jerrett Adams," he said after hesitating a moment.

"You mean T.J.," I said excitedly, short of breath from running up the stairs. "I'm looking for T.J."

"That's right, T.J. I think he's in the gym."

"Oh," I said. I tried to think of something to say. I certainly wasn't going to just turn and leave. I could only think of the obvious. "You're rooming with T.J. this year?"

"That's right. My name is Chris Thayer."

I didn't think to introduce myself. I stepped backwards and stumbled over a box of record albums. I tried to act calm but my composure was fast escaping, like the air from a punctured balloon. I felt schoolgirlishly silly and I'm sure I showed it. That this was Ethan Thayer's younger brother alone was enough to throw me. That this wispy, amber-eyed boy, the same age as me, sat on the board of the Thayer Foundation — yes, it was exciting. But there was more here than just good looks and a formal birthright. There was a palpable charisma, an immediate effect: a regal timbre in his speaking voice and a glowing coolness about him that filled the room, that trailed behind his movements like an invisible attendant.

He sat down on his desk and put his foot up on a Briarwood school chair.

"Be careful, guy," he said in delayed response to my near fall moments earlier. He smiled an almost forgiving smile of recognition, as if my stumbling and fretting were a commonplace reaction to his presence.

"You're Ethan's brother, right?" I said, still reeling and short of breath.

Chris ran his fingers through his matted yellow hair. "Yep. You know my brother?"

"Yes," I said. "We play guitar sometimes." I stood there shifting my weight from foot to foot, feeling silly and naked.

"You play guitar?"

"Yes."

"Cool. My brother has been playing a long time. Who do you like?"

"B.B. King. Guys like Son House."

"I know Son House. Cool. You like Steven Stills?"

I lied. "Yeah, a little." My eyes roamed over objects in the room that I recognized as T.J.'s — his tennis racket, his collection of folk music. "Well, I'm going to try and find T.J."

"Okay," he said, chuckling softly, his eyes lingering on mine as I turned to leave.

I stepped outside the room, and leaned against the wall in the hallway. The full effect of meeting Chris came over me slowly, as slow as a marijuana high. Suddenly it was deepest summer again. I felt as though I'd been sitting in the sun for hours. Though I'd been hyperventilating with excitement just minutes before, I walked slowly back to my room and took a nap.

※

I saw T.J. that night after dinner. He was standing by the bulletin board in the lobby of Chase Hall, intently poring over lists and announcements. I was so excited to see him I practically mugged him.

"Hi, T.J.," I said.

"Hi, Peter," he said softly. He gave me the impression of being deliberately cool.

"I met your roommate today."

"He told me. He said a black guy came over acting like a nut. I said that must be Givens."

"He said I acted like a nut?" I asked, faking a punch to T.J.'s stomach.

T.J. ignored my punch. "He said you were acting nervous."

I was happy to have made some distinct impression on Chris, even a bad one. I stopped and took a good look at T.J. His face was summer-reddened and his brown hair was lighter than I remembered. He was taller, but no heavier. He looked very handsome; just the slightest touch of manliness had begun to show in his features, though he still looked very much a boy. I grinned, remembering our sex from the spring before. I figured he knew what I was thinking, but he just looked at me curiously.

"Did you have botched brain surgery this summer? You have this retarded look on your face."

"My summer was terrible," I said matter-of-factly. "I'll tell you all about it later. Tell me about your roommate."

T.J. shoved a pushpin into the bulletin board with his thumb. He concentrated on the pushpin and didn't look at me. "His name is Chris," he said, and walked away.

✻

I saw Chris Thayer again the next evening at the Headmaster's Tea. Mr. Chase had invited a group of seniors and juniors to a dinner celebrating the completion of his new house. T.J. told me he was also invited, and so was Moonshot Lewis.

I left my dormitory around six o'clock and walked down the winding road at the school's entrance, through the woods to a clearing near the base of the hill. A year before this space had been a parking lot for school-owned vehicles. I stood for a moment and conjured up a memory of a gravel lot littered with oil cans, a dented green shell of a school bus, and piles of firewood stacked against ancient, rusted mechanical equipment. Now a neat, small wing of the Headmaster's new house jutted abruptly out of the woods. The wing extended into a square white mansion, large enough to hold at least twenty rooms, still partially hidden on its sides by trees and brush. Two students were standing by the back doorway. I walked past them and found my way to the dining room.

It struck me with distinct intensity now how different this world was from the world I'd been in only two days before. There were several faculty members there with their wives, including Dean Press and his wife and his daughter Lisa. Mr. Chase greeted me warmly and welcomed me back, beaming. Mrs. Chase held out her hand and murmured a tentative welcome. I never thought Mrs. Chase liked me.

The faces at the party seemed bright. There were a lot of teeth, and lots of fluid, proper chatter and restrained laughter. The laughter seemed inhibited, like a small child under a parent's watchful care, not allowed to wander into the street or stray too far from home. White skin blended with white, gray, blond, or light brown hair into a cream-colored collage. I felt a pang of antipathy, a bit of haughtiness, having endured my brother Malcolm's criminal rampage. I had seen more of life, I thought — I was street smart. But stronger than this pride or minor resentment was my desire to fit in here, my desire to escape. I waded into the sea of white. Something happened to me in those first few minutes. It was as though I forgot everything as quickly as it happened. I forgot what I felt the moment I felt it. Or maybe I didn't feel at all, but I'm sure I must have, I just forgot it — instantly. The wires had been pulled; I had become disconnected from some deep organic truth I would not accept.

The Headmaster wanted to speak separately with the Fifth Formers before dinner, so we all gathered in his study. Mr. Chase gave us the traditional welcome back, and then revealed his "true purpose," which was to convince us all to apply to Dartmouth, his alma mater. He introduced his friend and college roommate, Miles Trefir, a professor of history there. Mr. Trefir showed slides of the campus and told us how much he loved the traditions of Dartmouth, the same traditions, no doubt, he claimed, as Briarwood.

I couldn't concentrate on Mr. Trefir's talk. Chris Thayer was seated across from me, and my attention was drawn fiercely to him. He was twitching restlessly, the fingers of one hand pressed against his lip, the other hand cupping his elbow, as he shifted through a cycle of momentarily comfortable positions on the couch. He looked handsome and bored. His wide, quizzical eyes scanned the Headmaster's study like spotlights. "He looks just like a prince," I thought.

Afterwards we gathered in the dining room. For dinner we had lobster in white sauce and a chef's salad plate, followed by peach tarts and Earl Grey tea. I sat next to T.J. and Moonshot. I'd never realized the two of them were such good friends. They seemed to have a lot to talk about, so I kept quiet and enjoyed my meal. Chris Thayer was seated at the corner of the table, next to Mrs. Chase, who was monopolizing his attention.

Mrs. Chase was usually a stark, unnerving woman — small, brittle, and bony, with watery blue eyes that presumed dominance. With me she had always seemed, behind her grace, suspicious and disapproving.

Tonight, however, she appeared thoroughly won, both charmed and slightly awed by the Thayer heir. Chris flawlessly managed table talk with the adults at his end of the table. His voice was soft and regal and his manners facile. A crinkly, wincing smile — ambiguously mocking but decidedly charming — kept flashing into his face throughout the meal.

After dinner, we were given a tour of the house. Mrs. Chase led us through a maze of short hallways and tucked alcoves to the northern wing of the house, which looked out spectacularly over the Green River valley. Then we walked back around through several interconnected rooms. These rooms — mostly meeting rooms and guest quarters — were draped and painted in beiges and grays, or black and white, and scantily adorned with pieces of white porcelain and small oil paintings, all by the same artist. The paintings were all similar — white-capped, faceless maidens in telling, quiet poses against streaks of yellow and green plant life. Mrs. Chase told us that the rooms on the first floor would be kept in readiness for visiting parents, school trustees, and guests. The Chases and their two daughters lived upstairs.

After the talk we were served cocktails on the patio. I had a melon punch and circulated through the faculty to make small talk. I'd come to pride myself on my ability to sustain conversations with the faculty. I was so sincerely absorbed by whatever utopian ideal we were trying to enact, out there on the patio, that I'd disconnected from the truth that this was painfully vapid, and must have seemed equally so to whatever adult I'd cornered and trapped into playing his masterly role. I even ambled up to Mrs. Chase, whom I usually avoided, to make small talk. I secretly must have wanted to pump her for information about Chris Thayer. Or at least to share with her our mutual, evident fascination with him. She glowered at me through her watery eyes, and I went to get some more melon punch. I noticed T.J. and Moonshot were standing out on the grass, still giggling.

I had to go to the bathroom, so I stepped away from the party and back into the house. Chris and his brother Ethan were together in the Headmaster's study. Chris was nodding, and Ethan was whispering into his ear.

I walked past the study to the bathroom. When I came out, I got lost and wandered down a hallway and then past a staircase. I turned a corner randomly, and I'd come in a back door to the Headmaster's study. Chris was alone in the study now, seated on a beige, tweed couch that matched the color of his corduroy pants. His legs were crossed at the knee, and he was fiddling with his shoestrings. His eyes were vacant. I stood for a moment and watched as he sat back and nestled into the corner cushion. Seated at an angle he seemed almost invisible, lost in the soft lamplight that reflected off his skin and yellow hair.

"Are you coming back outside?" I asked.

"No, it's too boring." I sat down across from him and sipped my drink.

"You going to Dartmouth?" he asked, grinning as if the suggestion were absurd.

"Maybe. My name is Peter."

"T.J. told me. Peter Givens."

"Your roommate is insane, in case you haven't noticed yet."

"I've heard that."

"Where's your hometown, Chris?"

"My hometown?" He stirred as though he didn't understand me. "Oh, Pound Ridge, New York. Ever hear of it?"

I told him I had. My friend Mark Fix kept his horse at the stables in Pound Ridge.

"I used to work at the stables. I bet I know his horse."

I tried to laugh at this but couldn't. I was irritated because decorum required that I restrain my seething curiosity. My impulse was to tie Chris down and dissect him. "Did you know T.J. before coming here?" I asked.

"No."

"The reason I ask is you called him Jerrett yesterday instead of T.J."

"We have some mutual friends. I must know his family from Martha's Vineyard or someplace."

"His father's name is Jerrett Adams."

"T.J. is — yeah, he's kind of interesting. I'm glad I have him for a roommate."

I smiled blankly when he said this. Chris had a quality that seemed to slow down my reactions and, again, I had the feeling that I was basking in the sun. We were quiet for a moment. I was afraid I was boring him. Just then T.J. and Moonshot barged noisily into the study. Moonshot sat on the couch next to Chris. T.J. sat on the arm of an easy chair, then slid down into the seat.

"What are you guys doing in here?" asked T.J.

"What's up, buddy?" said Chris, perking up at the sight of his roommate.

T.J. was a little breathless. He tossed his head back and ran his hand through his hair. "I can't believe Givens is giving up a chance to suck up to the faculty."

"What were you guys laughing about out there?" I asked.

"VCPs," said Moonshot.

"I was telling Ron this house was bogus, all these rooms for the VIPs. So he says, 'Where are all the rooms for the VCPs?'" T.J. was talking to all of us but looking straight at Chris.

"Virgin Cherry Poppers," said Moonshot.

Chris looked surprised for a second, and then smiled. "I definitely need to check into the VCP room."

"You better check in quick, 'cause there won't be any left when I'm done," said Moonshot.

Chris got excited. "Sorry, guy, but you're looking at the East Coast all-time champion cherry popper. And I already have my reservations."

"Chris, this is my buddy Ronnie Lewis," said T.J. "We call him Moonshot. Moonshot, this is Chris Thayer."

Chris turned and shook Ronnie's hand. "How did you get the name 'Moonshot'?"

"It's a long story," said T.J.

Just then Dean Press came into the study. "Fellas, you can either join the party outside or head back up to campus with me, okay?"

"Yes, sir," we all said in unison. We got up and said good evening to the Chases. Then the four of us piled into the dean's station wagon and rode back up to our dorms.

※

That night I lay awake thinking about Chris. He'd surprised me at the dinner, horsing around with Moonshot and nodding out at the Headmaster's talk. Ethan would never behave like that. But Ethan would never have been kicked out of Whitehaven, either. "Very curious," I thought.

The two brothers were a picture of sameness and contrasts. Even at dinner I'd observed the same courtliness in Chris I'd always known in Ethan — a grace not so much natural as learned, thoroughly rehearsed and dispensed with a throwaway ease. Though Ethan was thinner, his hair darker and his jaw more square, there was between them a clear fraternal likeness, variations on a visual theme I found attractive. Both had small, tightly packed bodies, doe-like amber eyes, and a fullness in the nose and lips that gave a cream-puffy sweetness to features that would otherwise be bland.

I whispered his name aloud as I lay in bed. Christopher Thayer. Christopher *Blackwood* Thayer. I loved the pomposity of Chris's full name as I'd read it on the school roster. But I loved even more the incongruity of that old English resonance matched against this sporty boy in corduroys and desert boots, this unassuming scion who told dirty jokes and ducked out of boring parties. I decided that I liked Chris very much. *Christopher ... Blackwood ... Thayer,* I whispered again, before I rolled over and fell asleep.

✻

Classes started the next day. T.J. and I were in French class together, along with Moonshot. The three of us sat together in the back corner of the classroom, where Moonshot and T.J. continued the joint regression into infancy I'd noticed at the Headmaster's Tea. French, for some reason, was very funny to Moonshot. He burst out laughing whenever our teacher Mr. Boit asked him to recite. It wasn't long before T.J. and I were infected with Moonshot's contagious silliness. Mr. Boit was disgusted with us. He labelled us the "Diminished Triad" and took every chance to berate our performance. I'd never misbehaved in class before, ever in my life.

I tried out for varsity football and made it, to my pleasure, having put on ten pounds over the summer. More to my surprise, I was elected to the student council when the Fifth Form voted for class officers. Giddy from this first taste of voter approval, I began planning my political future. I imagined becoming a United States Senator, then accepting appointment as the Undersecretary of State. I started reading the *New York Times* to stay abreast of global affairs. I became intolerably grim and wise, until T.J. poured Pepsi-Cola over my head and told me to knock it off. After a week I got bored with the *Times* and forgot all about going into politics.

I saw Chris Thayer everywhere on campus — on the athletic fields, in the hallways of the Academic Center, or reading a magazine in the Common Room. In the library, he'd sit with his shoes off and one leg hung over the edge of his chair, dwelling for an hour on a single unturned textbook page, too long to be paying attention. He caught me watching once, and shook his head in mock agony. On the touch football field, Chris ran and played with a loping stride. He'd spin on one foot and bounce the football hard on the grass whenever he made a catch. Once I stepped on his ankle by accident, shearing his soccer cleat and sock half off his foot, and he became furious. "Look where you're going, Givens," he half cried, half commanded as he hopped like a pelican to the sidelines. Five minutes later he was back on the field, laughing and trying to knock me over. Outdoors, Chris seemed happier and livelier than he ever did indoors.

※

Three weeks into the school year, Mr. Chase announced Briarwood Beautification Day. Classes were cancelled, and the students were organized into cleanup and landscaping details. Chris Thayer was on my detail, and so were Keith Hanson and another black student named John Shepherd. Our team's job was to pull up weeds and chop the overbrush in the woods behind the athletic fields. It was a cool, clear morning, a perfect day to spend in a Connecticut forest. We were to work in pairs, and as we lined up to get our work tools and lunch bags I shoved my way past Gorilla Waxton to make sure I would work with Chris.

"Hey, watch it," said the Gorilla, shoving me back.

"Go take a bath, Waxton," I said. Chris turned and yawned, with his hands in his front pockets.

"Come on, guys, it's too early in the morning."

We all climbed on the back of a truck, and Dean Press drove us into the woods west of the soccer fields. Chris and I got off at the old Cushing cabin, a restored school monument that had been built by the original owners of the Briarwood land. Around the cabin was a four-foot-high wall of layered brick. Behind it was a tangled growth of dead white pine.

"These weeds grow in between the bricks, if you let them," said Mr. Press. "Then water gets in there and freezes in the winter, and splits the bricks apart. You guys chop all this weed off the bricks, okay? Get all the green off and rake it up. And then cut down all that whitewood in that clearing. It's dead and dried out, and there's too much risk of fire. I'll be back at twelve o'clock to see how you're doing."

Dean Press drove off towards the fields. I started cutting right away, but Chris sat down on a rock.

"Take it easy," he said.

"Press will be back to inspect in three hours." I looked at the green growth on the bricks and the huge net of whitewood. "We got a lot of work to do."

"I'll bet there's bees in that deadwood. You better be careful."

"Ain't no bee catching me, man. I'll break the sound barrier getting out of here." Chris laughed and picked up his cutters.

We worked steadily for an hour and cleared off the weeds from the bricks. Then we started to work on the deadwood. The sun came out high around eleven o'clock and it began to get warm.

"What are we, slaves?" said Chris, wiping his brow with his shirt sleeve. "They must think this is the Dark Ages, putting us out here like this." He took off his plaid woodsman's shirt, then pulled off his cotton t-shirt, struggling for a moment to get it over his head. "That feels better," he said. He wiped the sweat off his chest with the bundled-up t-shirt. He looked at me serenely for a moment. "Why don't you take off yours?"

"I catch cold easily," I said.

"You're just a pussy."

Dean Press came back around noon and inspected the bricks. "Don't leave those weeds scattered on the ground like that. Rake 'em up," he said. "Then finish up with that deadwood." He went into the Cushing cabin as Chris and I started raking the weeds. In a minute he came back. "Okay. I'll be back around four with the truck and we can haul it away."

"See you later, fartbag," Chris said as the dean drove off. He turned to me and let out a brattish, braying laugh. "I need a break," he said, throwing down his rake.

We stopped and took drinks from our water canteens, then opened our lunch bags. The kitchen staff had packed ham and Swiss cheese sandwiches and oranges.

"T.J. says you and he are really close," said Chris.

"Yeah, I guess so."

Chris looked off into the woods. "I think T.J. is really cool. He's an individual, you know. He's too excitable. But I like him. I think he'll go places."

"I think he's nuts."

"He told me you're on Honors all the time. And student council. What are you, Joe Prep or something?"

This wasn't what I wanted to talk about so I changed the subject.

"I was thinking about you last night, Chris." I spoke before I realized what I was saying. Chris registered no response to my more intimate tone, so I continued. "I remembered I met your father once. He was on a panel at Convocation my freshman year."

"You met ol' Henry?"

"Did your father go here?" I already knew the answer. I'd practically memorized the entry for Chris's family in *Who's Who in America*. Henry Thayer, Chris's father, was an investment banker and an alumnus of Briarwood. The Thayers were English Catholics who came to the United States in the 1800s.

"Yep. My father, my grandfather, my brother Ethan. My cousin might come here too."

"You're a real Briarwood family." Chris's eyes glazed over, and he looked lost for a moment.

"Let's get back to work," he said.

We chopped and cut and talked for the next couple of hours. Chris had a lot of things on his mind and he was in the mood to talk.

He talked about his past summer. He'd worked on a fishing trawler off the Maine coast. He described full days under the white sun, fish scales and nets, red raw hands and hard, sweaty work. I tried to imagine working on a fishing boat, but could only put part of the picture together.

We spoke philosophically about politics, about school, about love and sex. "Why do men love their ugly wives more than sexy pinup girls?" he asked. "Sure, they'll ball the pinup girl, but they love their skinny wife with no tits." Chris thought sex was all in the mind. I thought it was in the nuts. Although Chris thought student council was a joke, chapel was a joke, even sports were fun but still a joke, he took grades seriously. He jokingly predicted he'd beat both me and Barrett Granger for first in the class. He told me mathematics was a leisure interest of his father; at home, Chris was quizzed in the calculus over family dinner.

We bumped into each other once, and without thinking I leaned into his bare skin and stayed there for a long three seconds. "Get out of my way, Givens," he said, smiling and pushing me away with his elbow. In his mind he'd turned this drudgery of chopping deadwood into a sport, a contest between us.

Chris dropped his cutters on the ground. "I'll be back. I have to take a leak." He went behind a wide oak tree about ten feet away from where we were working. I could hear the tinkle of his belt buckle, and then the hiss and splatter of piss on crisp leaves. "Oh, that felt good," he shouted. His voice was flat and dry, like a foghorn. There was silence, then a long, louder yell. "Pete, come over here," he said after another pause.

I couldn't see him behind the tree. I dropped my cutters and walked towards his voice. Chris was standing with his back to the trunk. He still had his dick out, and was shaking away the last drops. Even after he was dry, he stood there holding it between his fingers.

"I wish there was a girl out here. I could really use some head." My mouth went suddenly dry. Chris was looking at something off in the trees, and didn't notice the hard look I could feel on my face. Before I could say anything, he tucked his dick away and zipped up his pants, then leaned back and propped one foot up against the trunk. He was breathing deeply and slowly and had a nervous smile on his face. I was frozen with nerves, standing in leaves.

"You want to smoke a joint?" he said. He pulled a thin marijuana cigarette out of his wallet.

I had never smoked pot before. I'd gotten drunk on beer at T.J.'s house, but I had always been afraid of drugs. In prep school, smoking pot was the equivalent of a capital crime. I could count the number of times Dean Press had announced a boy's expulsion for doing drugs on campus. But I was so taken in by Chris now, with his small, smooth chest, his hard breathing, his foghorn voice, the puddle of his urine in the grass at his feet, and now this conspiratorial offer, that saying no to anything he suggested was probably impossible. "Okay," I said.

I didn't like the pot. It made the sounds in the woods much louder, and I started worrying about mountain lions. It took my mind off Chris and onto Cady Donaldson and my brother Malcolm back home. We went back to cutting, and I worked even harder, hoping the exertion would push the pot out of my bloodstream. Chris said almost nothing too, and when he spoke now, it was in almost breathless whispers. He kept looking up into the trees. "The birds are cool," he said calmly. "When I smoke and I look up at a bird flying, I feel like I'm right there flying with the bird."

Keith Hanson and John Shepherd came walking through the woods with shovels on their shoulders. Keith spotted Chris and me, turned right, and started to walk out of his way, then turned back and came towards us. He stared at me blankly, blinking behind his thick glasses.

"You guys through?" I said.

"All done," said John. "We had to move all these rocks that were damming up a stream out that way." John pointed southwest.

"Great. Now you guys can help us," said Chris.

"We did our jobs," said Keith angrily. "You're not going to make us do your work for you."

"Just joking, guy," said Chris.

"I'll see you at dinner, Keith," I said. Keith and John walked off towards school.

"Jesus, I was just joking," Chris said after they'd disappeared.

"I think he expected me to work with him today."

"You'd think he owned you or something."

10

Chris and T.J. were a natural match as roommates. They came to breakfast together most mornings and sat and talked and laughed. One morning they had a food fight. Chris poured salt and pepper into T.J.'s hot chocolate and T.J. smeared mustard onto Chris's blueberry muffin. I saw them walking across the quad one afternoon, only inches astride of each other. T.J. did nothing but smile quietly. Chris, by contrast, was very animated, very much at ease.

In November was the Fall Cookout for the Fifth Form. There they were again! Off to themselves, Chris sitting with his legs crossed on the grass, T.J.'s arms wrapped around his knees, one loafer kicked off and dangling from the tip of his foot. There was a faint smile on T.J.'s face, a shade of tenderness over his eyes. He sat in a deep repose, as though with one deep breath he could have passed right through the earth as easily as sand through a sieve.

I was sitting with Keith Hanson at the cookout, eyeing the roommates from behind a tree. I wasn't worried that they'd catch me spying. The two of them were entranced. Their talk was flowing smoothly, punctuated by winsome gestures — a tossed grass seed, fingers whipped through brown or yellow hair. Chris did most of the talking. Chris was the only boy at Briarwood who could make T.J. keep quiet.

"What are you looking at?" asked Keith.

"Uh, nothing," I said, startled. I looked back at the two roommates.

"There's a fly on your hot dog."

I sat up and shooed away the insect.

"You're thinking about something. What is it, home? Your brother?"

"No," I said with irritation. Keith was annoying me now. I gave him my most dour, squint-eyed glance — a shot across the psychic bow — and then looked back around the tree. T.J. had rolled over on his stomach and smudged his yellow shirt in the grass. Chris was struggling to chew down too big a bite of hamburger. He coughed and his face turned red. "You pig," I heard T.J. say.

"It's nothing," I said to Keith.

"I'm getting another hot dog. You want one?"

"What?"

"Do you want me to get you another hot dog?"

I didn't answer. Chris and T.J. had stood up and were collecting their paper plates and plastic ware off the grass. They dropped their trash in the garbage bin and started walking together towards Chase Hall. I followed with my eyes as they walked up the back stairs to the infirmary wing. It seemed, for some reason, inevitable that Chris walked up the stairs first. When the door closed behind them, I turned and was surprised to see Keith frowning at me.

✺

I was terribly curious about the two new roommates. I had to take a closer look, so I went over on Saturday afternoon to give T.J. a guitar lesson. My stepfather, a big fan of Son House and Robert Johnson, had taught me guitar years ago. T.J. played guitar a little but wanted to learn more. We'd planned for months to practice together, but had procrastinated until now.

T.J. was seated on the edge of his mattress when I walked in. Chris was lying flat on his bed, reading a book and listening to the stereo through headphones.

"Hey, Pete," said T.J.

"Hey, Pete," echoed Chris.

"How's the guitar coming?" T.J. asked.

"Listen to this," I said. I sat next to T.J. on his bed and played a tricky blues-ragtime guitar figure I'd just learned.

"That's cool."

I played the song again slowly so T.J. could follow. "Now it's your turn," I said.

T.J. took my guitar and fingered a few basic chords. "Here, let me show you," I said. I put my left hand around T.J.'s to walk him through the melody. He relaxed and let me control his hand. His fingers were soft and hot, as I remembered. He breathed on my cheek when I moved closer.

"Show me again," he said into my ear. I glanced at Chris, who was nodding his head to music and concentrating on his book. Then I grabbed T.J.'s hand more firmly and pressed his fingers into the guitar's fretboard. My elbow was resting on his stomach now. I placed my right hand against his waist for balance. I could feel his flesh sliding under his cotton shirt. I looked up again at Chris, who was still reading and ignoring us.

"That looks a little tough for me," T.J said, looking too at Chris and moving away from me on the bed. "Maybe next year."

"We'll get there, T.J." I took back my guitar and put it aside.

"Have a seat, Pete," said T.J.

I sat down on a giant blue futon on the floor. "What are you guys doing tonight?"

"I'm going to the dance at Sarah Waters School. You want to go?" T.J. asked.

"I'll pass. The girls at those dances aren't exactly that hot." My standard excuse to escape the merciless boredom of acting straight.

Chris pulled off his headphones and sat up.

"Look who's back from outer space," said T.J.

"What are you boring Peter with now, T.J.?"

"The dance tonight."

"Those dances are for bozos. I go home to my girlfriend when I want to get laid."

"Right, Chris," said T.J. "Tell us about your imaginary girlfriend in Pound Ridge. The girl nobody has ever seen or heard of." Chris put his headphones back on and stretched out on his bed.

"You guys are just like husband and wife," I said.

"Chris is okay. Except he keeps leaving my record albums out of the covers." T.J. spoke loudly so Chris could hear him under his headphones.

"Your records stink anyway," said Chris. "All that pussy folk music." T.J. rocked backwards on his bed and smiled a very private smile.

Chris pulled off his headphones again. "You know why T.J. is going to the dance tonight, Pete? 'Cause he's still looking *desperately* for his first lay."

"Actually, I'm looking for my first blowjob from this guy named Chris." Chris threw his book at T.J., hitting him in the shoulder. T.J. started laughing. "Come on, Chris. Do me."

"Sorry to disappoint you, but I'm not into giving head."

"That's not what Duncan Roth told me." Duncan was a weird little bookworm in the Sixth Form who was reputed to be queer.

"I got the solution, T.J.," said Chris. "You can find one of those immigrant women who needs to get married to stay in the country. She'd still have to be pretty desperate." T.J. turned to me and shook his head and smiled as if he was in bliss.

I decided I'd seen enough. T.J. was too excited for a serious guitar lesson, and I wasn't in the mood for horsing around. I left the two roommates trading insults and hurling sneakers across their room.

※

The Milburger Dormitory, where Chris and T.J. lived, was at the far north end of the campus. It was a large, gray brick building, recently constructed, designed more fancily than the older dormitories. I lived in the old Greylock dormitory, which was near Milburger around the corner of the main lawn. Keith Hanson also lived in Milburger, in a single room two doors down the hall from T.J.

As much as I liked T.J., Keith really was my best friend. Ever since Third Form, we'd spent most of our free time together. And we were more than just social buddies. Keith and I spent hours in mutual psychoanalysis, trading dark Freudian secrets, trying to shock each other with ruthless self-excoriation. One night we'd confessed our greatest fears. Keith feared graduating from engineering college and then ending up a bum on 125th Street in Harlem, his useless degree in his back pocket. "If that happened, I'd kill myself," he said. I confessed that I was worried I was turning out socially odd. I was too moody, and my sense of humor tended to the bizarre. I had to double-check my jokes before saying them aloud to make sure they weren't too weird. Keith agreed that I was strange, but said this was okay because I could still function in day-to-day life.

Keith and I were cofounders of the Briarwood Black Student Union, which we modeled loosely after the Black Panther Party for Self Defense. Keith was the actual founder, lobbying the faculty for a black students club room and convincing them that we weren't actually race terrorists. He devoted great energies to the BSU, I thought, to deflect the charge that he wasn't really "black" because he came from Long Island.

As cofounder, I was dubbed the Minister of Information. My duty was to foment the black cultural revolution by writing articles for the school newspaper and organizing drama and music programs. For our yearbook photo, the BSU posed in black berets and raised fists. Keith's room became de facto revolutionary headquarters, and the black students on campus gathered there to listen to music and play cards.

Working together in the BSU, Keith and I became very close. We got together in New York in the summers, spending days at Jones Beach. The summer before, we'd walked for hours along the shore, and I'd barely made it back to catch the train back to the city. I was planning on going to law school, and I offered to draft Keith's engineering contracts and construction tax shelters when I got out. Of course, Keith was straight and I was gay, so there was a limit to our friendship. While Keith would jerk his head around to look at girls' behinds on the street, I was more interested in keeping my Popsicle from melting, or scanning the hairless armpits of the boy who'd sold it to me.

Since the start of the new school year, Keith had become more militant. I figured the politics were just going to his head, but he was noticeably less friendly to the white students. I was really surprised when he snapped at Chris in the woods on Briarwood Beautification Day. When the three of us were assigned to the same dinner table, Keith pretended not to hear when Chris asked him to pass the salt or the milk. Later he told me that the Thayers were corrupt capitalists who financed apartheid in South Africa.

Keith had made his dislike obvious, so I was surprised when Chris started coming down to Keith's room to visit when I was there. I had no idea what Chris thought he was doing. Keith wouldn't speak to Chris at all. Needless to say, I felt the tension, and I didn't say much either. At first Chris just sat quietly, mentioning that he liked soul music or that he respected Martin Luther King, Jr., and watched as Keith and I cracked jokes or made plans for the BSU.

Chris didn't appreciate the cooler treatment I gave him around Keith. He'd interrupt us in too loud a voice, or frown at me and leave. One Saturday evening, he was determined to get my attention. He danced in his underpants to the Aretha Franklin record playing on Keith's stereo, repeating over and over a rhythmic little two-step he'd mastered. Then he plopped himself on Keith's bed and interrupted our conversation.

"That was a great football game today, Pete," said Chris. Varsity football had beaten Trinity-Charles with a fourth-quarter touchdown, though I'd spent most of the game pinned under the elbows of a two-hundred-pound offensive tackle.

"You go completely *borneo* on the football field," Chris went on.

"Pete's always been a wild man on the inside," Keith said. "The quiet man with the hidden wild streak." Keith was always quick to analyze my brain for me. In this case, he was right. For me, everything was a matter of permission. On the football field, I had permission to lose control. I exploded in fury when the other team scored or when our team made a bad play. I hurled myself through the air to make kamikaze tackles. I really am lucky I never broke my neck.

"A wild streak, huh?" said Chris. "We have to bring that to the surface." Chris was rolling comfortably on Keith's bed now, inspecting his body, looking over his shoulder at hard-to-see places. He circled his thumb and middle finger around his wrist, then ran his forefinger along his arm as though measuring himself for a suit.

"I can't stand being so small," Chris murmured. "I need to put on about twenty pounds. What do you think, Pete?"

"Don't worry about it," I said. "You look okay to me."

"Pete," Keith interrupted. "How are we going to raise money for the BSU?"

"You think so, huh?" Chris jumped in, keeping me on the subject of his body.

"Sure," I said. I liked Chris's body. It was small and compact, like a miniature halfback, except his muscles were hidden by a smooth layer of baby fat, so that he resembled a dish of pudding. I didn't want him to gain weight.

"I should lift weights and get really big," said Chris.

I turned away to talk business with Keith, but Chris continued to distract me. He sat up on the bed and pretended to hold a movie camera in his hands, peek-a-booing through one hand and circling the other in the air as if rolling the film.

"How does it feel to be famous, Mr. Summus?" he asked from behind his invisible camera. "Mr. Summus" was Chris's new nickname for me. "Summus" was the Latin term the school used for high honors. Chris was in a silly mood, and he might have been stoned. He lay back on the bed and started making funny, incoherent sounds with his mouth. His front tooth was chipped from a soccer accident, and his lips were thick, almost Negro thick, which made him speak sometimes with a slight, alluring lisp.

"I love the way you nailed that guy on the kickoff. You speared him with your helmet. Wham!" Chris lunged upwards on the bed with his hips. "I bet you sterilized the guy."

Chris was beginning to embarrass me. He and Keith were ignoring each other and talking to me as though this scenario made sense. I tried to carry on two conversations at once, but it wasn't working. I couldn't keep my eyes off Chris, who was now practically doing a striptease on Keith's bed. Chris sensed he was winning me away and became more animated. He rubbed hard between his toes with his fingers, then lay still on his belly with his head on Keith's pillow, facing me. "Mr. Summus," he repeated several times quietly. His cooing repetition of my nickname — air squeezing past chipped tooth over bitten, pursed lips, his head snuggled brazenly in a strange boy's pillow — was almost a sex act in itself.

Chris turned over on his back and beat on his stomach like bongo drums. He snapped the elastic band on his underwear with his thumb, then snapped it again harder, then again, raising the elastic band inches above his waist.

"My nuts hurt," Chris said, smiling at me and tugging at his balls. "I think I need a nut transplant."

"Too much sex," I suggested. Keith let out a strained laugh.

"Not enough sex," said Chris. He pulled at his balls again, and ran his fingers under the bottom edge of his shorts. Then he hooked the two front flaps of his underwear with two fingers each and pulled the flaps apart.

"Looks like a clit, doesn't it?" My heart jumped. Without thinking, I raised my head to get a better look at the opening in his underwear. All I could see was a patch of blonde pubic hair. I craned my neck even farther to peek. I didn't mind Chris's antics at all now. I didn't mind his rudeness, and I didn't mind that he was embarrassing me. As Chris explored the suggestive potential of boys' briefs, I almost forgot that Keith was in the room.

Later, at a school dance, I realized Keith knew exactly what was going on in his room. We were drinking punch with Nancy Lane, a thin blond girl from our sister school, Sarah Waters. Nancy had seen me playing basketball earlier. After the game, she'd complimented me on my "legs." At the dance, when Nancy told me, "I want to get to know you better, Peter," I reacted as if she'd asked me for directions to Ireland. Keith told Nancy not to bother. "You don't know Pete like I do," he said casually. I guess I had been kind of obvious.

※

Two days later, I was walking with T.J. to French class. It was close to Thanksgiving, a very cool time of the year in

Connecticut. I had on my wool-lined windbreaker and was still shivering, but T.J. wore just a gray wool sweater under his blue blazer. The cold didn't seem to bother him. He was in a rare, quiet mood, distracted by some intensely private thought. I kept glancing at him, trying to catch his eyes, but he avoided looking at me, looking off over the slope of the hill, towards the chapel. I, too, was thinking hard.

I was wondering about T.J. and Chris. After his exhibition on Keith's bed, I had to wonder whether Chris was gay. When he pulled open the flaps of his underwear, I'd almost fainted. Could Chris not have known what he was doing to me?

And all those jokes between Chris and T.J. about blowjobs and Duncan Roth. I wondered. Was Chris crawling into T.J.'s bed at night, and T.J. wasn't telling me?

I was fascinated by the possibility. T.J. and Chris together in bed was the sexiest sight I could imagine. I visualized a tangle of cream-colored arms and legs, a head sticking out of either end of the pile. At least with me and T.J., you could always tell what belonged to whom.

T.J. wanted Chris to screw him. I could tell. I didn't mind. I was intrigued by the idea. I thought then that it was all about Chris, but I know now it was really about T.J. My feelings for T.J. were stirring quietly inside me — germinating like life inside a seed pod, not yet strong enough to push out and show bright, sparkling green. Chris had touched T.J. in ways that I had not, and didn't want to. It was T.J.'s strength I craved, just as I craved Kelly's softness. But the thought of someone else, of Chris, finding the little girl inside of T.J., the softness behind his strength. I wasn't just curious. I wanted it to happen.

I know this now, but at the time I didn't know anything. I just felt — curious, fascinated, affectionate. For a moment, my body was flooded with fondness for T.J. A ball of warmth circled inside me, rose quickly, and burst into my face in an unrestrainable smile. T.J. saw me smiling and turned towards me, curiosity in his face.

"Why was Thayer kicked out of Whitehaven?" I asked.

"Drugs. Sex. They caught him in bed with his housemaster's daughter."

"He told you that?"

"Yes."

This was disappointing but not conclusive. Better the housemaster himself, I thought. "I saw the two of you walking together yesterday. You looked like you were in love, T.J."

"Get out of here."

"You get out of here. You had this big, dumb smile on your face. You almost looked shy."

T.J. looked at me briefly and then at the ground.

"He came into Keith Hanson's room the other night in his underpants," I went on. "Boy, did he put on a show."

"What kind of show?"

"Rolling around on the bed, sticking his hand down in his shorts."

"And you liked it?"

"Sure I liked it."

"This is a strange conversation," T.J. said.

"All my conversations with you are strange."

We walked in silence for several yards. T.J. was still looking at the ground. "Would it bother you if I was in love with Chris?"

"No." I paused for a moment. "Maybe a little." I thought for a second of what T.J. was getting at. "I don't think of you and me as lovers. We're just friends who fuck each other."

T.J. slowed down and lagged a few steps behind me. He looked puzzled, as though he were trying to figure a math problem in his head. He squinted his eyes, looking hurt.

For a moment I felt burned, as though I'd cheapened myself. I wondered how well I knew T.J. There were things at work in him, feelings churning inside that I didn't know, didn't understand. I realized I'd been taking him for granted. My simple, sexy, happy little imp. And the one to take all the risks. In a flash it hit me — I wanted T.J. to seduce Chris, like he'd seduced me, so that I could then sleep with Chris. Now I was sorely embarrassed. I felt like a swine.

I'd never thought of T.J. needing anything, let alone me. I didn't want to deal with this new complexity, with him hiding thoughts and feelings from me, or making demands I couldn't meet by simply surrendering to him. "Come on, T.J.," I said. "We're gonna be late for French."

※

I started going to Chris and T.J.'s room as much as possible. How could I stay away? Chris and T.J. were the two cutest boys at school, superstars of sex, and it was amazing to see the two of them together, sprawled out on their beds or carousing and carrying on. If I was lucky I might catch Chris coming from the shower. He wasn't shy about being nude, and he never hurried to get dressed. Moonshot Lewis lived upstairs in Milburger, but often came down to be with us. We sat around listening to T.J.'s stereo and talking about sex and sports and which masters we thought were assholes.

T.J. didn't bring up the matter of us being boyfriends again. He didn't seem bitter or mad at all, he was as friendly with me as ever. I was relieved, but not because the idea of being T.J.'s boyfriend didn't appeal to me. It just made me vaguely nervous. Why did I act so strange with boys? I thought about my weird, confused behavior with Cady Donaldson. And my unreasoning dislike of Barrett Granger, my freshman roommate. I'd hated Barrett as soon as I met him, and I realized now it was only because, living in the same room, he was too close to me. As much as I liked T.J., there was still a certain distance I had to keep from him, perhaps from any white boy. And so I was relieved to see T.J. falling in love with Chris.

Still, I wondered whether T.J. wasn't heading for trouble with Chris, who remained a mystery as far as being queer or not.

Chris and Moonshot talked about girls all the time. Sometimes they were very silly. Big boobs, watermelon breasts, Titty City, deep dish pussy pie. It didn't matter to me. I was still meeting Kelly in the gymnasium attic, and I still went off to T.J.'s house once or twice a term, so I didn't need sex with Chris or Moonshot. It was enough just to be with them and to look at them in the shower, and they were both accommodating.

Except for some curiosity when I was twelve, I'd never really thought about girls. When Nancy Lane practically asked me to sleep with her, I reacted as if she'd asked me to jump off the roof. I really thought it was just that silly a question.

T.J. had slept with girls, at least so he told me, but he'd never been in love with a girl. I think it bothered T.J. that Chris slept with girls. He always turned quiet when we sat around joking about sex. That's how I could tell that T.J. was falling in love — he was jealous. Jealousy is the *sine qua non* of love.

Spending more time with T.J. and Chris meant spending less time with Keith Hanson. Since Keith's room was two doors down the hall, he could hear us in T.J.'s room making noise. Sometimes he would walk by the door and look at me with disapproval. Once he complained that the music was too loud. Chris snapped, "So what?" but T.J. got up and turned the music down.

Keith cooled to me noticeably. When I sat with him and John Shepherd in the dining hall, he would look away from me, and try to exclude me from the conversation. He started talking more and more about "black identity" and "the black struggle." He managed to get these words into any conversation I had with him.

I was mad at Keith for giving me this attitude. I liked my new group of friends. I still wanted to hang out with Keith and John, "the Brothers," as they called themselves. But I didn't like being pushed. I felt freer with Chris and T.J. They had no expectations of how a black kid should act. If my hair was combed out of style, they didn't notice. If I acted like a nerd, they didn't care. I was free to be my weird self, and they just assumed it was normal for someone from Harlem.

Besides, I was changing. I started to like the music Chris and T.J. played. T.J. liked folksingers and acoustic rock, like Bob Dylan and The Band. Chris liked heavy metal — the James Gang and Blind Faith. I liked both. The blues-based acoustic music was soulful and authentic, but the hard acid rock was just plain fun, like going to an amusement park. Moonshot said it all stunk, but I could tell he was starting to like the fluid, razored wildness of electric guitar. Chris worshipped all the great guitar players. He called them by their first names, as though he knew them personally. Eric, Duane, Ritchie, especially Jimi. "You have to realize, it's a tradition," he told me. "It's more than music, it's a whole cultural lifestyle." We argued about our favorite bands, and our least favorite. The transvestite rock star Alice Malice brought unanimous hoots of derision, especially from Chris. "I hope he ODs on his estrogen shots," Chris muttered venomously. T.J. and I, though gay as Christmas trees, saw no connection between sucking dick and wearing women's clothing.

※

Winter came, and with it winter sports. I warmed the bench for varsity basketball. I couldn't dribble or shoot, and I fouled everyone who came near me. Chris and Moonshot came to all my games, I think just to embarrass me. They piled into the top bleachers and yelled at the coach, "Put Pete in!" I scored one basket all season long, and Chris and Moonshot went wild in the stands, stomping the wooden bleachers until they shook, and yelling Indian war hoots. I was so embarrassed, I could have drowned myself in the water bucket.

T.J. played squash, a racquet sport I had never heard of before coming to Briarwood. Chris explained to me that squash was "a game for fruits named after a fruit."

T.J. invited me to one of his matches. The squash courts were in an old unheated shack behind the gymnasium. I didn't understand the sport — two players swatting a tiny black ball around a dusty, white cubicle — but I enjoyed watching T.J. play so hard to win. I had never seen him so serious and competitive. T.J. was good at squash. His legs weren't very strong and his knees barely bent when he moved, but his reflexes were fast and he could control his racquet and make trick shots. He was seeded number two on the squash team and won more than half of his matches. He won the day I came to see him play.

Chris was a star on the hockey team. Just like his brother, he was terrifically tough for his size. Hockey players twice as big would smash Chris into the boards, shaved ice would fly, skates would cross like knives. Chris would pick himself up off the ice and impossibly score the winning goal. The biggest game of the season was against Whitehaven, Chris's old school. Chris scored two goals and got into a fight with Whitehaven's goalie. The overweight goalie pushed Chris's face down and pulled his jersey over his head, but Chris drove forward frantically on his skates and they both fell over into the hockey net. Moonshot, T.J., and I hollered, "Kill 'em, Chris!" from the side of the rink. After the game, Chris skated straight to the locker room. I wondered why he didn't stay on the ice to talk to his old teammates.

※

Have I told you about Moonshot Lewis? His real name was Ronnie; we called him Moonshot because, in certain biological aspects, he resembled almost literally a Saturn booster rocket.

Moonshot was a miscreated black boy whose face, from certain angles or depending on your mood, might strike you

151

as deformed. To me, he looked like a genetic mutation. His chin was elongated and triangular, his eyes blurry quarter-moons. His body was long and thin, all smooth black muscle, arms, legs, and torso assembled with a deranged sense of disproportion, as if collected from different bodies. Moonshot was ugly, but intriguingly attractive: an overall effect of demonic sleekness and tight-twisted reptilian power.

I suspected Moonshot and Chris were doing drugs together. They seemed to have secrets, things they never told me or T.J. I watched in envy as Moonshot whispered confidential matters in Chris's ear at dinner, or ran off to Chris's house for the weekend. (If it wasn't Chris's house, then it was Shelton Buckey's, or Mark Fix's.) Moonshot was one of the most popular boys at school.

Ronnie and I were never that close. If we were ever alone together, we hemmed and hawed until Chris or T.J. got back. Perhaps he thought of me as a rival, or perhaps I reminded him, like a mirror, that he was black, and made him wonder what he was doing being friends with these two white boys. For whatever reason, Ronnie didn't talk to me much.

Still, I always suspected that he liked me. Something out of the corner of his eye, something subtle in his stare reached me, more like a radio signal than an expression. I felt at times a telepathic contact with something deep in Ronnie's mind, a not quite perceptible command to come to him and surrender. Perhaps the toxic chemicals or radiation exposure that had mutated his body had also gifted him with ESP.

If I could barely recognize Moonshot's hunger for me, it was because his lust was a quite different thing from T.J.'s. Moonshot just wanted to fuck me. My ass was the thing; my face and dick were superfluities to him. I learned from Ronnie that the sexiness of black and white were very different things, traveled along different wavelengths to separate regions of the brain. I felt warmly preyed upon when

Moonshot smiled at me in the shower, his lip curled upwards and his eyes, half-closed, angled downwards towards my rump. I imagined french-kissing his ugly face, and sucking him like a slave.

But I was too afraid to approach him. The feelings Ron aroused were new, harsh, scary. As long as he would allow it, I was satisfied to drop my bar of soap on the shower floor, bend over slowly, and glimpse Moonshot's vicious, imploding leer, upside down from between my legs.

※

This group of boys — T.J., Chris, and Ronnie — dominated my emotional life that third year at Briarwood. At the center of us all was T.J. Adams. He brought us all together. He loved Chris, he was Moonshot's best friend, and he was seducing me more profoundly at every turn. Though Chris had the most money, Moonshot the biggest dick, and I got the best grades, I really think T.J. was the brightest light among us. He had the most nerve. We were all reacting to him.

There was diversity and electricity in our little queer enclave. Together we formed an underground network of open and closed desires, affections, loves, and hurts. The separate facets of our homosexual matrix gleamed and receded variably, like points of light on a sparkling diamond, taking turns in prominence.

11

☀ It was a warm afternoon in the spring. Moonshot and I were in Chris and T.J.'s room, listening to records. Chris wanted to score from his drug connection in Pomfret, Connecticut, and he wanted us to go with him.

"I'm telling you we can make it."

"We'll all get kicked out, Chris," I said.

"No we won't. We go to dinner, right? After dinner, we cut down the hill behind the chapel and hitch into Hartford. We take the train to Pomfret, score, hang out all night. My friend will drive us back. We'll be back here before breakfast."

"Who's gonna be looking for us on a Saturday night?" said Moonshot.

"Right," said Chris. "And it's gonna be worth it, too. The best black hash and cocaine. Mix them together, whoosh, to the moon. Ronnie's going. Right, Ron?" Moonshot and Chris slapped each other's palms. "Come on, Givens. You're so straight. I thought black guys were supposed to have balls."

"I'm not doing cocaine," said T.J.

"Me neither," I said.

"So, come along for the adventure."

An hour after dinner we were on the train to Pomfret. It was getting near dark. Chris lit a cigarette and took a long draw. "You guys are going to really like Gusto, " he said.

"Who's Gusto?" asked T.J.

"He's my dealer. Gusto's a maniac. In 1954 he drove his Jeep onto the outskirts of an atomic test site in Nevada. The blast turned his hair white and took away his color vision. He went nuts 'cause he thought he was gonna die of cancer. So he bagged college, spent ten years in Japan, but he never got sick. He's been dealing hash out of the Far East ever since."

"He can't see color?"

"That's what he says. Everything is black and white. Says his hair used to be red, but now it's white."

"You sure he doesn't change into a giant purple monster at night?" I said.

"He's still waiting to mutate. He says it could happen any day."

Chris was seated across from T.J. in our railroad car. He shunted downwards and put his foot up on T.J.'s seat, between T.J.'s legs. He looked odd that way, with his raised desert boot and his shoulders shrugged as if he didn't have a neck.

"How you doing, buddy?" he said to T.J., shaking his cigarette ash between his legs onto the floor.

"I'm okay," T.J. said quietly. He leaned back and turned to look out the window. We were passing through thick forest. The trees seemed only inches away from the glass.

"I love riding on trains. This scenery is really cool, right?"

"Yeah," said T.J.

"Why won't you get high with me?"

"I just don't want to do drugs."

Chris flicked more cigarette ash on the floor. "We should have sex together. With two girls, I mean. We could get two babes, blow some hash, and ball them together in the same room."

T.J. smiled and flushed red.

"We're *roommates,* man," Chris said. "And we're going to be business partners in the future. We can do stuff like that. It's like being blood brothers. I know a cabin in North Hartford where we could go and do it. I know two girls, too."

"How come you know so many girls in this area, Chris?" I asked.

"I'm not like you dorks. I scout out my territory before I move in."

"Line 'em up and knock 'em up, right?" said Moonshot.

"And your own private sex cabin?" I offered.

"Damn straight," said Chris. "I'm a spoiled preppy brat and I want *everything.*"

Chris shifted up in his seat when he said *"everything"* and almost kicked T.J. in the testicles.

"Ooops!" said Chris, pulling back his boot.

"Hey, watch it!" grinned T.J.

"Sorry, pal." They looked at each other for a second. Chris rested his foot back between T.J.'s legs and they both relaxed into their seats. No one spoke for a minute.

"Damn, boy, I could use some pussy right *now,*" said Moonshot, grabbing his dick through his pants.

"So could I," said Chris blandly, dragging on his cigarette and likewise grabbing his crotch. He smiled at T.J., and a beam of red light from the setting sun mixed into the amber hue of his eyes for just a second.

"Gusto says you never really know a guy until you've watched him fuck. Then you get a sixth sense about him. You can read each other's thoughts."

"That's weird," I said.

"I think it's like a war thing. Martial philosophy. Gusto's been in 'Nam, Korea."

Chris moved his foot from T.J.'s seat and leaned forward. He put out his cigarette. "You want to try that, sometime, T.J.?"

T.J. didn't answer Chris. He just looked wanly out the window. We were passing over a huge wooded canyon with a rushing, shallow stream beneath. A man dressed in denim was standing by the side of the stream. I wondered what he might be doing there. On the horizon, the sun was hiding behind rust-colored clouds.

✳

Gusto lived in an old-fashioned white house surrounded by hedges. There was a wide lawn in front, and a dirt walkway went from the road right to the front door. It was dark when we got there, and I could see all the windows in front were lit with the curtains drawn. Our taxi dropped us off in front, and we walked around back. Chris knocked on a screen door.

A man in his forties with long brown hair came to the door. "Who are you?" he asked.

"We're looking for Gusto," said Chris.

"I said, 'Who are you?'"

"I'm Chris Blackwood. He knows we're coming."

"Yeah, he told me. Come on in."

He led us through the kitchen into the living room.

"Gus'll be back in a few minutes. Make yourself at home, fellas." The man went down a flight of wooden stairs to the basement.

The living room could have been a room in Mr. Chase's house. There was a black sofa and two loveseats, both covered with white flower-print upholstery. There were plenty of green plants. At one end of the room was a stereo with speakers as large as small refrigerators. From down in the basement, we could hear rock music playing.

We heard the screen door in the back creak open and slam shut. A man in his midthirties came into the kitchen.

"Gusto!" said Chris. As Chris had told us, Gusto's hair was white, cut short with streaks of faint yellow, as though someone had splattered drops of yellow dye on a white sheet. He was tall and thin and wore a white, slightly soiled sleeveless t-shirt, tight black corduroy pants, and brown boots. He had black and red cotton wristbands around each wrist.

"Thayer! I can't get rid of you, can I?" He threw a bottle of beer into the refrigerator.

"No way, Gusto," said Chris.

Gusto reached out to shake Chris's hand. "Good to see you, Blackwood." He turned to the rest of us.

"You guys are Blackwood's buddies?"

"This is Moonshot, T.J., and Pete Givens," said Chris.

"And you're at this Briarwood School now?"

"That's right."

"The *Briarwood* School. Whooeeee."

"I got one more year, then I'm bagging it," said Chris.

"I'm not going to ask about *Whitehaven.*"

"They caught me nailing this chick in the dorm. I was already on probation for drugs, so they asked me to leave."

"For getting a little pussy? They shoulda pinned a medal on you." Gusto winked at me and Ronnie. "How come they call you Moonshot?"

"It's a *long* story, Gus," said Chris.

"Oh ho," laughed Gusto. He put his arm around Chris's shoulder. "Let's go upstairs for a minute."

"Why don't you guys put on some music?" said Chris.

"Yeah, I'm sorry, fellas. Help yourself to the fridge, play my records. I got to talk to Blackwood here for a second, and then we can hang out. I want to get to know you guys."

Chris followed Gusto upstairs and the rest of us sat down on the loveseats. T.J. searched through the record bin and put on an Eric Clapton record. Chris came back in a few minutes.

"What's up?" T.J. said.

"Gusto's making a phone call. I got the stuff."

"Isn't he afraid of getting busted?" asked Ronnie, looking through the curtains.

"Not *here*. He doesn't keep anything big here. If they busted him here, it would just be a possession rap."

"He stores the stuff someplace else?"

"I'm not supposed to talk about his business," said Chris. Chris pulled a pipe and a chunk of black hash out of his pocket. He stuffed the hash into the pipe, lit it and drew a puff, then handed the pipe to Ron. Chris started playing an imaginary electric guitar.

"Clapton can *wail*. You guys want beers?" asked Chris, jumping up and going into the kitchen.

Gusto came downstairs. He'd changed into a black dress shirt and white jeans.

"You're T.J., and Moonshot, and Pete Givens, right?" he said, sitting back on the sofa and pointing to each of us.

"You got it right," said Ronnie, handing Gusto the hash pipe.

Gusto took a long draw on the pipe. "We're going to know each other before this night is over."

※

"How does it feel being radioactive?" T.J. asked Gusto. It was about eleven o'clock, and we'd been talking and listening to music for hours. Gusto and T.J. were sitting close to each other on the floor with their shoes and shirts off. Chris was asleep on the sofa, stoned from too much hash. Moonshot was downstairs with Gusto's roommate. I was sitting in a loveseat with my legs swung over the arm.

"Well, I thought I was going to die at first. I sat around for three years just waiting to turn green. My hair turned white. I used to be a brunet. First I got this long white streak in my hair. Then it all turned white."

"Bullshit," said T.J., chuckling.

"You're a wise guy, huh, Mr. T.J.?"

"You don't know the half of it," I said.

"I should call up some chicks. We could have an orgy," said Gusto.

"No, this is cool," T.J. said abruptly.

"What did the blast look like?" I asked.

"Oh, I didn't see the blast. I heard kind of a popping sound in the distance. I turned towards the pop, and I got hit by this big wind of hot air, and then the sky turned dark. Damn, I was a hundred miles away from the blast."

T.J. started shaking his head and laughing uncontrollably. Gusto looked at him wide-eyed, and then smiled tenderly.

"Didn't you see the warning signs?" I asked.

"Hell, I was twenty years old, I was stoned. I was getting into it, out there all by myself. I thought, just that much radiation" — he pinched two fingers together and closed one eye — "would make me a true mystic."

"I did something stupid like that when I was a kid," I said. "I saw *Peter Pan* on television, and I really wanted to fly, so I got this battery charger from my father's tool drawer. Then I cut off an extension cord and hooked it up, and plugged it into an outlet. I thought the extra power charge would make me able to fly."

"Jesus, what happened?" asked T.J. He was lying flat on his back now, with his feet crossed at the ankles.

"I blew out all the electricity in our apartment. I'm lucky I wasn't electrocuted."

"'Cause you thought it would make you fly," said Gusto.

"It's like believing in the Tooth Fairy," said T.J.

"Right," said Gusto. "When you're two years old you believe in the Tooth Fairy. When you're a little kid, you believe in Peter Pan. And when you're twenty, you believe two kilorads at a hundred miles will turn you into Carlos Castaneda."

"And when you're fifty years old—" I said.

"Then you believe the most outrageous shit of all."

Gusto turned and looked at T.J., and T.J. laughed. It was his most precious, pixie, Third Form laugh. I hadn't heard him laugh quite like that in two years.

❋

It was much later. Gusto trained a fish-eyed glare on me. "So what's your story, Peter Givens? Where do you come from?"

"New York City."

"Where you from, Mr. T.J.?" He poked T.J. in the ribs and T.J. pushed his hand away.

"Old Greenwich," he said, giggling.

"And you two are best buddies? What a trip."

"What makes you think we're *best* buddies? There's four of us here," I asked. T.J. looked straight at me as I spoke.

"Oh, I can tell," said Gusto. "You and him are the tightest in this whole group. I have a special insight. Or maybe ... just maybe it's T.J. and Moonshot that'll stick together in the long run."

I looked down at the floor and frowned. "Chris said you can't see colors."

"Metaphorically speaking, that's true. I see everything in black and white. No in-betweens. Like you, for instance, are you black or are you white?"

I was stunned and I didn't answer.

"You don't know, do you? Do you know who that is you're running around with, over there on that couch? That's the heir to the Thayer Foundation. Do you know who his grandfather was?"

"I know he was in the State Department."

"Deputy Secretary of State during the Korean War. We're talking serious, old, *old* money. That's some buddy for a black kid from New York."

"I can handle it," I said. I was starting to get angry.

"Sure you can, up in the snow-capped candy mountains at *Brriaarrr*woo-ood. But someday you're gonna be asked to make a choice. I can't see you, brother."

"I'm not worried about the future. I know I can deal with it."

"I can't see you. I can see you *now*, but in the future, no. 'Cause you're not black and you're not white. To me, you're invisible."

I stood up to go into the kitchen. "You want anything, T.J.?"

"No thanks, Pete."

"Don't stress it out, dude. I was just being poetical."

"No problem, Gusto." I went into the kitchen to get a beer.

※

When I came back Gusto was gone.

"Where's Gusto?" I asked.

"He went upstairs to make a call."

I sat down next to T.J.

"I think Chris was in on one of Gusto's orgies."

"Sounds probable."

"You think Gusto is queer?"

"I don't know. Maybe," said T.J., smiling to himself.

"Do you think Chris might be queer?" I asked in a hushed voice.

"You keep asking me that. No, I don't think so."

"Gusto was starting to touch me off."

"It's all right to get touched off. Maybe he's right."

I glared at T.J and then rolled over on my stomach. "He's not right. He doesn't know anything."

Gusto came running down the stairs. "All right, my little chickadees. Here's the good news. The 5:10 out of Boston gets into Pomfret at 6:30, arriving in Hartford at 7:45. It just so happens I'm heading north tomorrow morning, so I'll be happy to drop you off at the bus depot. Here's an alarm." Gusto put a wind-up alarm clock on the night table. "And if you guys oversleep, you're walking." He turned and headed back upstairs.

"Good night, Gusto," said T.J.

"Good night, Gus," I called.

"Come on upstairs if you want. Just don't forget to set the alarm for Blackwood over there."

"Stay with me, T.J.," I said after Gusto had gone upstairs.

"I think I'm going to hang out with Gusto."

"Please, T.J. Really, please."

"I'll come back down here to sleep."

"You going to let him fuck you?" I said brattily.

"If he wants to," he said, lifting himself up off the floor, and revealing a swelling in his pants. I wanted that swelling in my mouth so badly, I could have killed Gusto.

It really bothered me when T.J. went upstairs. I fretted and pouted until I fell asleep. I put two sofa pillows over my ears because I didn't want to hear if T.J. started squealing or crying out. This was the night it all began to change. Maybe it was the cold spring air and the warmth from the space heater Gusto had plugged in, or the aroma of hashish, or the drone of the King Crimson record that had played over and over since midnight. Maybe it was just the late hour. Watching T.J. on that living room rug, goofing and playing and laughing with Gusto, he changed from being just hot and funny and sexy, to beautiful, truly beautiful, and lovable. I thought of the pixieish hellion who had mellowed and saddened since our Third Form year, the hell-pack of charm who had made friends with my mother in seconds. I closed my eyes and dreamed of him. And it was a wonderful dream. Yes, I'm sure of it. This was the night that I fell in love with T.J.

※

We left Gusto's house early the next morning. My three friends slept most of the way home on the bus, but I was too turned on to sleep. I was sitting next to Ronnie, with my eyes on the erection in his pants. His dick kept heaving and shifting around on his thigh. It looked as though a gopher had burrowed into his pants and was searching for a way out.

Chris and T.J. were leaning against each other, asleep in the seats across from me and Moonshot. They were snoring lightly. Chris was curled with his face buried in T.J.'s shoulder. I noticed the back of Chris's hand was resting on the inseam of T.J.'s thigh.

We got into Hartford and caught a cab into Green River. We had breakfast at the Farm Shop and then walked the mile back to campus. There'd been a light rain overnight, and the road was wet and grainy.

"Shuffle your feet in the gravel," said T.J. "It makes your feet vibrate."

I tried it and liked the sensation. T.J. and I lagged behind, dragging our feet in the road.

"What a couple of touchholes," said Chris.

"Where was Gusto headed?" T.J. called after Chris.

"Bah-ston." Chris turned around and waited for us to catch up. Moonshot kept walking ahead. "You guys glad you went?"

"Yeah, pretty glad," we answered in unison.

Of course we were glad. We'd run off into the night like bandits, travelled across the state, partied with cool, drug-dealing hippies. We'd plumbed philosophical depths with the lunatic Gusto. As we walked towards school on that damp, gray Sunday morning, I felt closer than ever to my three new friends. If I had been alone, I might have cried.

✺

After our trip to Pomfret, I spent almost all my free time in Milburger. I stopped in to see Keith from time to time, but Keith was very cool to me now.

Like any pair of roommates, Chris and T.J. had their disagreements. Sometimes I thought it was amazing they got along at all. Chris's side of the room was always cluttered with dirty towels, baseball equipment, and sweat socks. T.J.'s bed was neatly made, his clothes and books all tucked away. His record albums too, unless Chris had left them on the turntable collecting dust. It seemed whenever I stopped by their room, Chris was reading sports magazines. T.J. was usually studying to keep himself on Honors. I never saw Chris studying.

Then there was the matter of money. Chris's family had more than T.J.'s. The Thayers were enormously wealthy, even by Briarwood standards. There weren't any outward signs, of course. T.J. was the one with the new stereo, the skis propped up in the corner of their room, the multi-featured diving watch. But consumer goods were hardly sound indicators of the Thayer level of wealth. Chris was unassuming about money, but he gave himself away through innocent remarks. When T.J. talked about his trip to the Whistler Mountain Ski Resort, Chris interjected, "Oh, yes, we have a house there," his tone casual as if to say, "Oh, yes, I saw that movie."

"Oh, I forgot, your family is so rich," T.J. retorted snidely. To me the difference between Chris's and T.J.'s family fortunes was meaningless, like the distances from earth of a nearer and farther star.

In their room, T.J. seemed cast in the housewife's role. Chris dominated T.J. in ways no one else could — teased him, commanded him, kept him up late. "Calm down!" Chris would order when T.J. became hyperactive. Chris didn't like his serenity disturbed, so he put a cap on T.J.'s bubbling energy. "I'm the boss of this room," Chris said bluntly one day; T.J. didn't argue, though he did pause and stare.

It began to bother me that Chris could dominate T.J. Before, I'd been intrigued, but now — I wondered if T.J. liked Chris more than me. If you loved someone, did you show it by being submissive? Wasn't I man enough to make T.J. feel like a girl? I could be submissive to T.J. because I still felt I owed him for my sex life and my social life. I might have waited years on my own before trying gay sex. Only T.J. had the right touch to get me over my shyness, I still believed.

Anyway, I didn't like the idea of my husband letting someone else push him around. Even if Chris was gay, he didn't love T.J. like I did. That was for sure.

One day when T.J. was out, Chris complained to me about his roommate.

"T.J.'s a moody asshole, Peter. He complains 'cause I keep him up late. And then he has these hysterical fits and starts running around like a two-year-old. Plus he's jealous, because I have a girlfriend and he doesn't."

"The guy has a gland problem, Chris. How many times have I told you?"

"He's becoming a real pain. And he does some really strange things sometimes. You think you know T.J., Peter, but you don't."

"But you guys are taking that house together in Nantucket this summer. How come you're doing that if you hate him so much?"

"I didn't say I hate him."

"But you're bitching about him so much, lately."

"Well, sometimes things happen. I don't know how that happened. He just asked me and I said yes." A haze fell over Chris's eyes, that sleepy, distant look that so enamored and intrigued me. "I guess the guy is okay."

※

Whatever Chris felt about T.J., T.J. was hotter for Chris than ever. When Chris pushed him around, T.J. glowed like a pregnant woman. When Chris insulted him, he was tickled into hysteria. His whole body seemed to swell and tingle when Chris was around. He became antsier than ever, tossing and turning on his bed, rubbing against his mattress, spreading his legs. It was as though T.J.'s whole body had turned into one big, fully erect sex organ.

Living with Chris was driving T.J. crazy. I just knew something had to go wrong.

12

※ Chris wanted me to meet him in the dining room. There was something important he had to tell me. We both were free first period, so we could take a late breakfast and have some privacy.

I knew something was wrong. When I'd seen T.J. at dinner the night before, he was pale and fidgety.

"Did Chris talk to you?" he'd asked.

"No. What's wrong?"

"Oh, uh, nothing. Nothing," he'd said and walked away in a hurry.

Chris had come up to me several minutes later. "Meet me for breakfast tomorrow. I have to talk to you."

"What's going on?"

"I'll tell you tomorrow. Meet me first period, okay?"

When I got to the dining room, Chris was sitting in the far corner with his back to the window that looked out on the infirmary. I came over with my breakfast tray and sat across from him. Behind him I could see the school nurse through white see-through curtains, up and about her early duties. Billy Green was there, I knew, healing from a waterskiing accident.

"T.J. is a *faggot!*" exclaimed Chris.

"Quiet down, Chris."

"He wants to have sex with me. He's a goddamn queer." Chris's face was screwed into a frown. He was pouting and exaggerating the thrust of his words. I could tell he was angry, but I couldn't tell just how angry.

"He came on to you?"

"We were getting ready for bed last Friday night. T.J. pulled off all his clothes. Nothing strange. I thought he was changing his underwear. But he sat on the bed like that for about five minutes. I know he's a little weird, I'm not worried about it. So I pull off my pants, 'cause I want to take a shower. When I get my towel wrapped around my waist, T.J. gets up, comes over behind me, and puts his hand on my shoulder. I'm in shock, right? I don't know what his problem is. So I just stand still and don't say anything. I half expect him to start crying, tell me his mother died or something. Then he leans his head against my back, and ... he *gooses* me. He goosed me naked. I tripped over my bed getting away from him. See?" Chris pointed down at his foot. "Look where I scraped my ankle. And he's just standing there with a *boner* on and this crazy look on his face." Chris was the one with the crazy look now.

I looked over my shoulder around the dining hall. One of the kitchen workers was frowning at us as he wiped off tables across the room. I couldn't tell whether he'd overheard Chris or whether he just wanted us to finish and leave. Chris went on talking, stage-whispering now in a quicker voice.

"Then he went to his bureau and took out a clean pair of underpants and put them on. He could hardly get them on over his boner."

I looked down at my Raisin Bran. It was starting to turn soggy. Why was Chris telling this to me? Didn't he know I was queer too? I began to feel nauseated. "What did you say?" I asked.

"What do you think I said? 'No fuckin' way, T.J. I'm sorry but no fucking way.'"

"Didn't he say anything?"

"He said he was sorry. He just got under his blanket and said he was sorry."

"Wow."

"You didn't have any suspicions? You've known him a long time. He told me you've been to his house."

I almost choked on a piece of toast. "No, I didn't."

"I'd heard a rumor about him in Martha's Vineyard. From somebody that knew he went here. But I figured, you know, innocent until proven guilty. Well, he proved himself guilty, all right."

I felt as if strong hands were squeezing my stomach like Play-Doh. Chris was talking almost breezily now. Expatiating on queers. After all his teasing. He's completely crazy, I thought.

"At first I was shocked, so I didn't mention it. Then I got really pissed off. I was sort of grossed out. It really bothers me—" His voice rose and quickened again.

"Chris, you shouldn't be telling me this."

He looked baffled. "Why not?"

"It's not going to do T.J. any good for everybody to know."

He sat quietly for several seconds, mulling the thought. "I guess not."

"Plus, people might say—" I paused, "—you led him on. Like they say in rape cases."

Chris rolled his eyes. "What a thought."

"Who else did you tell about it?"

"Nobody." I looked at him hard. "Just Mark Fix."

"Not your brother?"

"Hell no."

"Don't tell anybody else."

Chris seemed disappointed at my suggestion. "I guess you're right. If the guy has a problem, I shouldn't make it worse."

We sat quietly for a few minutes. I looked straight at him, but Chris wouldn't meet my eyes now. He just sat there, scooping and stirring his tea.

"You don't hate T.J. now, do you?" I asked.
"I don't know. I got pretty pissed off, Pete."

※

T.J. had fifth period off, so I walked over to his room. He was lying down with his shoes off and his arms folded across his chest. I walked over and sat on the edge of his bed.

"Did you talk to Chris?" he asked.

"He told me you made a pass at him."

"Yeah." He turned around on his side facing away from me, looking out the window. I waited for him to say something.

"Chris is a cockteaser," he said finally.

"I'll say."

"He makes it so obvious, and then he wants to pretend he didn't do anything. The guy lives in a total dreamworld."

"Chris said he told Mark Fix," I said.

"He told a lot of people. Everybody knows, Pete."

T.J. sat up on his bed and sighed. Then he smiled at me softly.

"How did it happen?" I asked.

"I don't know. I've been kind of dropping hints lately. Obvious hints. He went along. We were always kidding about each other's butts and things like that. He said he was so horny even I was starting to look good. He even told me he'd fuck me if I put on a pair of falsies."

"Jesus."

"I was getting ready to go to bed. And I noticed him staring at me. So I — I just froze. I felt really nervous. I thought he was going to make me. But he just keeps on looking right at me. Then he starts to undress. He takes off everything, and he's standing there for about five minutes with nothing on. Christ, Pete, he looks so good. I thought I was going to faint. I wouldn't even stand up, 'cause I thought I would just fall down. Then he turns around and shows me his butt, then he wraps his towel around his waist, but he's still looking at me in the mirror. So I went over to him."

"I don't blame you."

"I could just as easily accuse him. He wouldn't dare act like that in front of anybody else. He knows I like him, and he just ... I don't know, he fucks around with me."

"If somebody makes it that obvious..."

"Then on Saturday night, he came in really late with that girl Jenny from town. They woke me up when they came in, laughing and acting stupid. Then they started kissing and fooling around. She wanted to stop, but he kept, like, making her." T.J.'s face turned red. "He fucked her right in front of me!"

"Jesus!"

"God, Pete. I feel so bad. I don't know what I'm going to do." He laid his head down on his pillow.

"You want to go to lunch, T.J.?"

"Yeah, let's walk over."

T.J. and I took the grassy path behind Greylock House to Chase Hall.

"Chris is avoiding the room," he said. "He leaves in the morning and comes back for lights-out."

"He'll snap out of it, T.J."

"I don't care if he does."

T.J. stopped and pulled a blackberry off a bush. "I'm not coming back next year," he said. "I can apply to St. Christopher's. My dad went there. I'm sick of this school."

I didn't expect to hear this. My heart thumped once very hard. I didn't say anything more to T.J. I just went into a quiet panic.

※

The news about T.J. spread, but not like wildfire. Rumors like that made a lot of boys nervous, boys with their own secrets to keep, who couldn't repeat the story without stammering and flinching. Once Chris stopped talking about it, for most students it remained unconfirmed gossip, which was a commonplace occurrence. Almost everyone at Briarwood was accused of being queer at one time or another.

There was some trouble, of course. I overheard two Third Formers joking that if they struck out at Sarah Waters they'd stop by T.J.'s room. "We better check for gonorrhea on his gums first," joked one spritely cherub, his dental braces gleaming when he smiled. Third Formers! T.J. told me that when he came into the shower one day, all the boys glared at him and walked out at once, even one still covered with soap.

T.J. and Chris had a reconciliation, of sorts. T.J. told me all about it. Chris said they had to live together, so he would forget about it, but don't try it again, and the summer share was off.

I didn't know what to make of Chris Thayer. T.J. was right, he was seductive — in the woods, in the shower, on the train to Pomfret. Was it possible that he was just that sensual, just that friendly and open and free? Did a straight boy *have* to have hang-ups about his body?

And the cracks about oral sex. It went on all the time, it was a running theme at school. Homosexuality was a ubiquitous joke at Briarwood.

Chris had evaporated for me now, as a person. When I looked at him it was like looking at a ghost. There was nothing real there. Just like Malcolm when he came out of jail. I would have never imagined Chris's cruelty to T.J. Especially what he had done in their room with Jenny Richards. One day a group of us were sitting around Chris's room talking. T.J. was sitting at his desk trying to study. "Hey, Chris, who is this Jenny girl?" someone hollered.

"I met her in the Green River Mall," Chris said.

"You *made* her in the Green River Mall?" More cackling and giggling.

"So what are you, just mall buddies?"

"He mauled her in the mall." Snickers and guffaws.

"I'm balling her. I balled her last Saturday night."

"Where?"

"Right here in my room."

"Where was T.J.?"

"I don't know. You went out somewhere, right, T.J.?" said Chris. T.J. didn't answer, but I could tell from the blackened frown on his face that he'd been right there when Chris and Jenny had sex.

Chris had always ignored the fact that I was attracted to him. Even on the first day I met him, he must have known. He couldn't help but notice how my eyes lingered on his crotch, how I lost myself in his resin-colored gaze. Once he'd come into the athletic supply room naked except for his baseball stirrups. I froze at the sight, as though I'd been struck in the head. Chris looked ethereally beautiful, his body composed of long curvy waves of flesh, like slow folds of whipped cream. And his dick — it was thick and smudged; it looked nasty to me. It looked lazy and fat, well-fed and self-indulgent, sinful and piggish as it hung slovenly against Chris's angelic thighs. Chris didn't seem to mind as I looked then, or at other times. He just understood and ignored it. Perhaps he understood too well. I just couldn't figure Chris out.

❋

I was walking in from track practice when Chris caught up to me.

"You want to walk?" he said.

"Sure."

We detoured behind the tennis courts and sat down on a small, grassy slope that fully caught the setting sun. We didn't say anything for a few minutes, just tore up grass blades and ran our fingers through the dirt, looking out at the sunset. I was trying to decide what to say.

"You can usually tell, you know," I said.

"Tell what?"

"When another boy is looking at you in the shower, or across the dining hall. You know it's a queer look. It doesn't mean the guy is queer, it's just a part of him. Like a little voice inside he doesn't pay any attention to, but it still slips out every now and then when he isn't looking."

Chris didn't say anything. He frowned and squinted into the sun. I turned towards him and went on.

"You're going to tell me you never had any idea about T.J.?" I tried to sound skeptical. I didn't want to accuse Chris of leading T.J. on, but I wanted to drop a strong hint.

"What are you, an expert on queers?" he said, tossing a pebble down the hill.

I dropped my head between my legs and studied the ants scurrying in the grass. "I made it with T.J., Chris. I made it with him lots of times. Ever since last year." My breathing quickened. I was still peering at the ants. "I couldn't let you go on thinking it was just T.J. That would make me such a goddamn hypocrite."

"You made it with T.J?"

"Yes."

"Do you want to make it with me?"

I looked up at him. My heart was pounding hard. I looked down and saw the fullness in his crotch. "Yes," I said. He stood up on the hill. His dick was sticking straight up in his pants, and the tip of the head had pushed out over his belt. "Come on," he said.

We walked down the hill and into the woods. Chris pushed me against a tree, pinning me roughly against the wood. Chips of bark were scraping my spine. He shoved his pelvis against my stomach and ground so hard up against me it hurt. Tears were in his eyes, and his face was red. He sucked my face, my nose, my lips. He licked up and down my cheeks and in the corners of my eyes. Then suddenly he stepped back. He fumbled with his belt buckle, then dropped his pants down to his ankles. He had on a red, oversized woolen workman's shirt; his dick stood straight up, and the front of his shirt was draped over his cock like a tent. Chris stepped forward and pressed his face against mine. I fell down on my knees and put my head under his shirt. I'd just gotten in the head and half the shaft when Chris pulled back and it slipped out of my mouth. "No," he said. "Let's get behind the tree." Chris sat down in a crook between the tree roots. I kneeled down in front of him. "These leaves are scraping my ass," he said, smiling. I didn't answer. I couldn't think. My whole brain was focused on getting back to that dick. I felt like a starved wolf; I would have killed Chris right then if he'd tried to keep his cock from me.

I ducked my head back under his shirt. It was warm and moist under there. I could see the red shade on Chris's smooth belly button. It reminded me of how my brother Tyrone and I used to crawl under my mother's laundry rack and pretend it was an Indian teepee. It felt good to be in such close quarters, with the sun's warmth and shaded light filtering through the sheets and towels on the rack.

And I thought of the old-style photographer's tents in the slapstick cartoons. "Watch the birdy," the photog always said, and his explosive flash would blow up in his hands. I smiled at the thought, then the musk of Chris's groin hit my nose, bringing me back to the present.

I ate. I sucked. I made love to Chris's dick. I sniffed his balls, I chewed on his pubic hair. I burrowed under his nuts to sniff his butt. I tried to lick his ass, but my tongue could only reach the tips of the hairs, that were crusted with bits of dried shit. I licked them off and rubbed the grains of crud against the roof of my mouth. The taste sent my brain into the red zone. I put my arms under Chris's knees and lifted them over his chest.

"Whoa, calm down!" said Chris. I pulled my head up from under his shirt and looked at him. He pulled me towards him and french-kissed me sweetly. "Keep doin' what you were doin' before, okay?" he whispered in my ear.

"Okay."

"Wait a second," said Chris. He unbuttoned his shirt and threw the flaps to the side. Now I could see him smooth and naked from his collar down to his ankles. I started to feel dizzy.

His dick was half-hard now, lying straight down between his thighs. I cradled it in the crook between my nose and upper lip. It woke up and said hello. I nudged it with my nose. It rolled over and stretched. I tickled the head with my tongue and it pulled away. I looked up at Chris. He was smiling at me, with a keen glint in his eye, trying not to break up laughing. I licked the full, fat length. It swelled and turned to bone, and then relaxed. I sniffed the head, and it stood up on its own, clipping one side of my nose and snapping past it. Now it stood staring me in the face. I lapped it up backwards. It turned to bone again, flexed, and then softened and hooked forwards. I sucked on the head for two seconds and let it go. It fell backwards, rolled around in a circle, and came back straight in front of me. I looked at Chris and he laughed.

"Stop playing with your dinner," he said.

No more fooling around. I gripped as much as I could between my tongue and the roof of my mouth, and rubbed my tongue backwards and forwards. "Do that until I come, okay?" Chris whispered. It took a little while. Chris pulled his legs back and bent his knees to get some leverage, then started pumping up with his hips. Five or six violent bounces into the lips, "Oh Pete, *oh Pete!*" He knocked me backwards. Then a foghorn in the distance ... two short gasps, one long, straight stream in my face. What a mess! It was all over my shirt collar and probably behind my ear.

"Nice work, fellas." I looked up in time to see Dean Press lift his camera. The flash in my eyes blinding me. This can't be happening...

I fell out of bed and woke up. "Oh my god," I said aloud. I turned on the lights and looked at myself in the mirror. "I'm never going up to that attic with Kelly again."

13

So now I was having wet nightmares. I didn't need a psychiatrist to analyze *that* dream. I was feeling guilty. If I had half of T.J.'s nerve, I would have tried to make Chris, and now I would be the one getting the heat. But I didn't have to take that chance, because I knew T.J. would. And I let him. I encouraged him.

And Chris still thought I was straight — or at least his confused, ridiculous idea of straight. Confiding in me, expecting me to side with him against my own boyfriend. The whole business made me sick. It was just like T.J. to plunge me into an emotional mess by taking some impulsive, boneheaded action, totally outside of rationality. T.J. would have followed his dick into the Grand Canyon.

If I wasn't going to come out to Chris, at the least I had to stand by T.J. If I overheard anyone making fag jokes about him, I cursed them out or told them to shut up. "Why do you care about another guy's sex life? Maybe you're the one who's queer, since you're so *interested* in it." This was my standard, Machiavellian rejoinder, hypocritical, I know, but it worked.

I had to stay loyal to him, but to tell the truth I could have kicked T.J. He was making a mess of my social life. The four of us — Chris, Moonshot, T.J., and I — couldn't be friends together anymore.

And the Brothers and I were getting along worse than ever. Keith Hanson stopped asking me to help him with planning for the BSU. John Shepherd called me a bourgeois nigger, which was just short of being an Uncle Tom. I thought they were being unreasonable and they were full of shit, anyway. Talking as if they were the Black Panthers in prep school. The Green River Connecticut Liberation Army. I sat in T.J.'s room bitching and fuming and moaning about it.

"They're right," said T.J. "You're an Uncle Tom. I read all about it."

"T.J., I'm going to kick your ass if you don't shut up."

"Your friends are right, Peter. Gusto was right. Even Ashley Downer was right. Remember how you used to hate rock music? Now look at you. You're developing identity confusion."

"It's not really about race. It's about sex. I think they know I'm sleeping with you."

"You are a pretty obvious queer." *I* was an obvious queer? I could have hit T.J. in the head with a chair, but he was looking at me with a twisted, nervous smile. I remembered how much pressure he was under and I calmed down.

"Things like the weekends," I said. "They think it's weird. None of the Brothers like you, T.J. You're too prepped out."

"Maybe we should cool it."

"No, I don't think so."

T.J. tucked his foot behind my ankle. "I don't think so either."

※

Keith and John Shepherd came and sat with me at lunch the next day.

"Where's your boyfriend?" asked John.

"Don't bother me, I'm eating."

"I heard you were taking up tennis lessons."

"This isn't Nazi Germany, John. I can talk to whomever I want."

"Fair enough, Peter," said Keith. "No one is taking away your freedom of choice."

"Good."

"But you can't just ignore us, either. T.J. has a reputation. This homo stuff — that's whitey's thing. Black people aren't about that. You didn't come here to get your head turned."

"I think you better try minding your business."

"It's all the same thing," Keith said, looking at John. "Homosexuality, individuality. It's not how you feel inside that matters. It's how you're supposed to act on the outside."

"Boy, you sure seem to know a lot about it."

"That white boy can afford to do what he wants," said John. "We can't afford it. A brother with your education has to marry a sister and raise a family."

"Thanks, Malcolm Luther Muhammad."

"Now you're wrong, Peter," said Keith.

"I have a sister, and I'm helping her raise her family," I almost screamed.

※

I was angry and confused after lunch. I knew I shouldn't have said those things to John, but he made me so angry. At track practice I couldn't concentrate. I tripped going over a high hurdle and skinned my knee. In the shower after practice I saw Chris Thayer, not my favorite person by now. I turned away from him, remembering my dream, but he came to the sprocket next to me.

"Did you hear what happened to T.J.?" he said.

"What?"

"He got into a fight downtown. I heard he collapsed and he had to go home."

"What do you mean he got into a fight? Whose T.J. gonna fight?"

"Hanson and John Shepherd."

"You've got to be kidding me."

179

"They're in big trouble. They were with Press all afternoon. I think they're getting expelled."

I got dressed and ran over to the infirmary. The nurse told me T.J. had an asthma attack when Keith Hanson shoved him to the ground. T.J.'s parents had come and taken him home to see their family doctor. There was nothing I could do. The nurse assured me T.J. was okay.

That evening at dinner I didn't speak to anyone. I just glared at Keith two tables across from me. I wanted him to know how angry I was. I couldn't stop thinking of T.J. down on the tennis court our freshman year, his eyes tearing, his face scrunched and red. Crawling on his knees. I hated to think of him so humbled.

After dinner I took a walk out to the north end of the campus, the shortcut down the hill, and then walked back up through the woods. I needed the air and I thought the exertion might burn off my nervousness. I came up from the woods behind the chapel. There was a narrow strip of road there for cars to drive around. A pine log fence bordered the road at the top of the hill; just beyond was a steep drop-off into the dense woods. I sat on the chapel's back porch and tried to make myself cry.

I was almost able to. I wanted T.J. with me right then. I remembered how it was. I could feel him playing inside of me, awkward as a pony, jerking, free and happy. His arms locked under my armpits, or his hands grasping my shoulders, then squeezing tight, his breath in my ear when he came.

As the sun set, I walked back to my room. I spent the next several days in the sourest of moods, angry at Keith. And angrier at Chris. Now his lies and craziness were touching me directly.

❈

T.J. was away from school for a week. When he came back, I went over to his room to see him. He was furious.

"Shepherd and Hanson run into me downtown and they say they want to talk to me, white boy. I told them to get lost, 'cause they're fucking racists. Then they say I should leave you alone, that I'm trying to turn you, or corrupt your brother, or some shit like that."

"Corrupt their brother."

"What?"

"Corrupt *their* brother. Not corrupt *my* brother."

T.J. stared at me so hard I flinched. "Jesus, Pete, what did you say to those guys?"

"I didn't say anything. They were making insinuations, and I just goofed it off, made it a joke. I didn't actually deny it."

"They better get kicked out or I'm gonna sue their families. They'll be living on nickels and dimes for the rest of their lives."

"Sue them, not their families."

"Damn it!"

"How are you, T.J.?"

"I'm all right. Fucking asthma complications. I forgot to take my medication. Keith pushed me down and I lost my breath. It hit real suddenly, it felt funny. Not like my normal attacks. I really couldn't breathe, Pete."

"They must have scared you. And all this stuff with Chris. It must have made you nervous."

"It was a good thing Moonshot was there. He called the ambulance."

"Moonshot was with you?"

"That's what set them off. First you, then Moonshot, like keep my hands off the black race or something. God, they are crazy."

"You should try to keep calm, T.J."

"Yeah. Thanks for coming by, Pete. Why don't you split, I'm gonna try and sleep now."

"Go ahead and sleep. I'll stay here and read."

T.J. slept for two hours. I tried to read from his Shakespeare book, *A Midsummer Night's Dream*. Thoughts of

Moonshot and Chris and Gusto were running around my head and I couldn't concentrate. I stopped reading to watch T.J. sleep. I listened to his slow, quiet breathing. For a second, I wanted to hit him with the heavy Shakespeare book. But my twinge of anger passed. T.J. woke up coughing and went into the bathroom for a glass of water. I waited until I knew he was feeling better before I asked him.

"Are you fucking with Moonshot Lewis?"

"I think you'd be able to tell. I can still walk, can't I?"

"I think you're fucking him."

"Pete, you're acting like we were engaged or something."

"Well, aren't we boyfriends?"

"Boyfriends? When did that happen? You told me we're just friends who fuck each other."

I remembered the stupid expression I'd coined, back when Chris first came to school. I decided to keep my bright ideas to myself from now on.

"Well, now I want to be boyfriends."

T.J. stopped and stared at me and smiled. Many hours of thought were in that smile. He was wiping his hands with a towel, and he'd taken off his shirt. "I'll think about it," he said.

※

Keith Hanson and John Shepherd were placed on Final Probation. Final Probation meant they lost all their junior privileges and couldn't go off campus. Blink wrong and they'd be expelled. Dean Press announced at assembly that they wouldn't be expelled because they didn't know about T.J.'s asthma. All that had happened was some overly aggressive roughhousing, lost tempers which didn't warrant expulsion. No one had mentioned the reason for the fight, not Keith or John and not T.J. I looked over my shoulder after the announcement and saw Keith staring at me. There was an eerie look on his face. I frowned at him and turned away. I thought he blamed me for the whole trouble. I wondered why Keith didn't mention queerness to defend himself.

After assembly I ran over to T.J.'s room. "What did you think of Press's announcement?" I asked him.

T.J. was lying on his bed in shorts, reading the paper. He spun around and sat up. "I was in the infirmary. What did he say?"

"They're both on Final Pro. Hanson didn't know you have asthma, so he wasn't expelled." I sat down at T.J.'s desk. "Hanson is a Nazi," I said. "He's always talking about walking in lockstep, the group over the individual."

"I thought you and Keith were best friends."

"Not anymore."

"Because of me?" He looked at me suspiciously. "How could he know I was off my medication?"

"It's not just because of you."

"Chris and I were friends, and then he turned on me like a snake. It's supposed to mean something, you know. You don't just drop your best friend. You give him a chance."

"You don't understand," I said. "You're white."

"Moonshot doesn't have this problem. He still gets along with Hanson."

I was badly stung. "So, fuck Moonshot if you want to so bad. He's your hero. He saved your life."

T.J. put his head down on his pillow. "I wish this hadn't happened, Pete."

"I know. It's fucked up."

"That's not what I mean. I wish it hadn't happened to you. It's going to make you worse."

"What are you talking about, T.J.?"

"I'm talking about what Gusto said. About seeing black and white?"

"Don't talk to me about Gusto. You went upstairs and fucked."

"We didn't fuck. We stayed up all night talking."

"Really? I thought you went upstairs to have sex." I walked over and sat on the bed next to T.J. My eyes could have lit up China when I heard this news.

✺

Keith approached me in the Common Room in Chase Hall that afternoon.

"I have to talk to you."

"Go away, Keith. I think you're dangerous. You attack T.J. You talk like a Nazi."

"Nothing happened to him, did it?"

"I didn't say anything happened. I'm just telling you we have nothing to talk about."

"You choose the white over your own kind. That's wrong."

"I don't want to hear that, Keith. We used to be friends, right? But now you're into totalitarianism. That makes me so fucking mad."

"That's it, isn't it? It's just some kind of rebellion. You're not really a homo. You just refuse to love sisters. Like a little boy who won't eat his carrots. It's a Freudian thing."

My head started pounding. "That did it, Keith."

"I know how your mind works, Peter. Remember how we used to talk?"

"That did it, Keith. You are too weird."

"Don't say that. Don't fucking say that."

"All this bitterness. You're a racist! Why don't you just leave this school? You don't want to be here."

"I have a right to be a racist. The white man killed my brother."

"What?"

"I said the white man killed my brother."

"What?"

"Cliff is dead!" he screamed. "He got shot by a white cop. They pulled him over, 'Get out of the car,' discharged the pistol right into his head."

"I'm sorry. You never told me."

"You're right I never told you, you house nigger."

"When did it happen?"

"It happened after Christmas. He was driving back to Colgate. An accident, they said. Mistaken identity. Someone else in a black Chevy. The same old bullshit."

"Why didn't you tell me about this?"

"Why should I talk to you? You probably think it was justifiable homicide."

"No, I wouldn't—"

"And now you want to suck whitey's dick. And the worst ones, too, none of the cool ones. That T.J. is right out of the Roaring Forties. And that snot-rich bitch Chris Thayer."

"Chris Thayer?"

"Yes. You think I'm not watching. You're so obvious. You wouldn't sit with us at breakfast, you wanted to suck blondie's white ass so bad." I was stunned. Keith sat down on a sofa. He looked exhausted.

"I'm really sorry about your brother."

"Yeah, you're sorry." I reached out my hand but Keith pushed it away. His eyes had filled with tears. I didn't know what to say.

※

I spent that evening in Keith's room. It was the first time we'd really talked since winter. My head was spinning. No one was acting like I expected anymore. T.J. didn't trust me. Chris was a delusional closet case. And Keith hadn't even told me when his brother died.

I had only met Cliff Hanson once, at the Whitehaven game our Third Form year. He had a good sense of humor, I remembered, and he'd made my mother laugh. Cliff was the same age as my brother Malcolm. Malcolm. My head always started hurting now, whenever I thought his name.

"We come up here," said Keith. "We come up here with these white people, but we're still niggers. We can get shot in a drop. In a drop, Pete. Shot for nothing."

185

"What's fucked up is, if Cliff really were a criminal he probably wouldn't have been shot. Criminals know how to act with a cop. My brother Malcolm told me. No false moves, don't give them any lip. If you're innocent, you get nervous or you cop an attitude about your civil rights."

"You go on believing that, Pete. If they want to shoot, they shoot."

"My oldest brother Jackson died. I told you about it, right? The worst part was the effect on my mother. It was horrible."

"I thought my mother was going to have a stroke. She still might. Then it's double murder."

We sat silently for a moment. Keith got up and put a Quincy Jones record on his stereo. "This album was my Christmas present from Cliff," he said. A perfect trumpet voice filled the room. Very spare, very dark and sweet. Keith tapped his fingers in time with the drummer. Then he turned and leaned against his desk.

"So you're really, what, gay? Homosexual."

"I've always known that you knew."

He came back and sat down next to me.

"I'm in love with T.J., Keith," I said. "But he's not in love with me. He used to be, but not now. I think he's in love with somebody else."

"T.J.," Keith snorted. "I can't see it."

"He stood up for you, you know. He was mad at first, but then he stood up for you. You complain about stereotypes, but then you stereotype him because he wears yellow pants."

"You guys should be careful. You really are obvious, you know."

"The real freak is that Chris Thayer. Don't repeat this, Keith, but Chris likes guys as much as I do. He just can't admit it to himself. He led T.J. on."

"He won't accept that he's gay?"

"Right."

"Just like you won't accept that you're black."

I stared at Keith for a moment that felt like an hour. I didn't have the energy to object to what he had said. I closed my eyes and just listened. Quincy Jones was holding a long note, impossibly long, longer than that note was meant to live; in the end it just evaporated. I opened my eyes and looked at Keith again. Maybe I was judging Chris too harshly.

※

Two days later Keith got into a shoving match with Dean Press. Keith had insisted on eating his roast chicken with his fingers ("like we do in my house," he said) instead of with a knife and fork. When the dean objected to his table manners, Keith called him a fat white honky pig. He was expelled from school immediately. His mother and father drove up to school to get him. I went over to his dorm room to help him pack.

"Well, Keith, you'll go home, you'll get it together. You've got so much talent. The world is just waiting for you to kick its ass."

"We all get what we want," Keith said. "Like you said, I didn't want to stay here."

"I can't believe you tried to punch out Press. Remember how we used to kid about him?"

"'Don't mess with Press.'"

"Remember when he kicked out all those guys for smoking cigarettes? Just for smoking cigarettes."

Keith imitated Dean Press in his best Paul Robeson baritone. "'You've got five hours to pack your bags and *leave.*'"

"Yeah, Press is a bad dude."

Keith's mother came into the room. She was older and heavier than my mother. She was dressed in a black dress with a colorful, black-and-pink kerchief around her neck. She looked around the room and picked up tidbits Keith might have forgotten, like his hairbrush or a photograph of his family. She looked very grave and she kept quiet until Keith spoke.

"Mom, you remember my friend, Peter Givens."

"Hello, Peter Givens," she said. I looked at her but I couldn't speak. Mrs. Hanson picked up a photograph of her dead son and stared at it. My heart muscle squeezed. All I could think of was my first night at Briarwood, and my mother making friends with the boy I had fallen in love with.

❋

I wondered for days if I had betrayed Keith. I'd been blind to the fact that he was hurting. And I had drifted away from his friendship, so consumed was I with Chris Thayer, and more and more attached to T.J. Still, I wasn't worried about Keith. After I explained to Mr. Chase about Keith's brother being murdered, he changed his expulsion to a voluntary withdrawal to keep his record clear. Keith would go back home to public school, then off to engineering college. I was more worried about what T.J. thought of how I had treated my best friend.

I was worried because betrayal is the worst, the most bitter feeling. The wolf in the field, you can fight. But the evil that sneaks into your bed and crawls up your skin, the two-faced troublemaker, the unknowable liar, the evil that destroys truth and trust and faith — this gave off the most repellent stench. I knew how T.J. valued honesty. And I knew how he felt about Chris — who had led him on and betrayed him. If he thought I was a traitor to my best friend, I knew he would never love me.

Part 4

14

T.J., Ronnie, and I worked in Briarwood's summer school program for disadvantaged youths from Hartford. Chris Thayer was offered a counselor's job, but turned it down to spend the summer on his family's ranch in Wisconsin. I taught music, T.J. was a teacher's aide, and Ronnie worked with the grounds crew. We lived on campus and had our pick of rooms in Milburger. There were also girl aides on campus, from Sarah Waters School; they stayed in Chase Hall across the main lawn.

It was grand to be with T.J. in the summer. Most nights after dinner we relaxed on the front stoop of our dormitory, drinking beer and playing music. T.J.'s brother had sent him a tape by a gravel-voiced roustabout named DT who sang folk ballads and bluesy rock and roll songs. T.J. really loved DT. One night he kept me up until morning listening to his records over and over. When we found out DT was giving a concert in Stratford, T.J. invited a group of us to go to the concert and then spend the night at his summer house in Point O' Woods.

Six of us squeezed into T.J.'s Peugot sedan and drove down the interstate to Stratford on Saturday night. Besides T.J., Moonshot, and me, three other aides were in the car — John Bragg, Susie Blomberg, and Meg Buckley. The trunk was loaded with six-packs of beer. Ron and John smoked marijuana on the trip. Neither T.J. nor I smoked pot.

We parked outside the concert arena and got drunk before we went in. It was always the same when T.J. drank. After a few beers a dumb, dizzy smile would spread across his face, as if he'd downed a quart of Tennessee whiskey instead of three Budweiser tall boys. Then his head would start to weave, as if attached to his body by a rolling ball joint.

"I'd say I got a buzz on now," he always said, proud of achieving a state of brainlessness.

Ronnie and John, drunker than the rest of us and stoned, were standing with arms and shoulders interlocked, parodying DT's boozy song-style: *"Poor old lover man DT, ooooh-oooooh-eeeee-oooowwhhh!"*

T.J. joined in. *"Hey, baby. DT coming to getcha."* The girls sat on the hood of T.J.'s car and stared at us curiously, like cats.

We met T.J.'s brother outside the arena. Jeff Adams had white-blond hair and eyes like brown pecans. He was sparely built, like T.J., a little more muscular. Jeff was there with his girlfriend Gina, who looked sexy in cutoffs and sandals. I instantly knew that I liked Jeff. He was handsome in a more distinctly male way than T.J., thinner and rougher in the face. Jeff was the serious outdoors type, serene compared to his baby brother, but I could sense in him the same inner charge of energy. In T.J. it burned like a flare; in Jeff it was a slow blue flame. T.J. had told me things about his brother — that he was honest and a good skier and popular with girls. Jeff and I chatted about Harvard, where he was a junior. T.J. saw us talking and smiled at me. I smiled back as brightly as I could — I wanted him to know how excited I was to meet his brother. I handed Jeff a beer from the backseat of T.J.'s car. He tossed it down and then we split up. Jeff and Gina had third-row seats, and ours were up in the back.

DT sang like the devil that night. His voice speared the darkness on killer ballads about heartless women and drugs, and his band staggered and crunched their way through old-style rock and roll songs. Since we couldn't get six seats in a row, T.J. sat with Susie and Meg two rows in front of John, Ron, and me. John and Ron hollered and hooted through the show. T.J. kept looking up at us during the concert, as if he were missing the best fun.

After the concert we drove about thirty miles east to Point O' Woods. The Adamses lived in the summer on a modest spread of land surrounded by a moat of trees and thick brush. An old-fashioned, black-panelled house stood about thirty yards back from the road. Behind the house about fifty yards back was a large pine log cabin. Meg and Susie, both friends of the family, went into the house. The rest of us carried the remaining beer to the cabin to party for a few more hours. We played the Allman Brothers' *Idlewild South* album and continued drinking.

Besides DT, T.J.'s favorite group was the Allman Brothers Band. The Allmans featured twin blues rock guitarists who improvised guitar counterpoint that reminded me of the Bach Double Concerto. T.J. and I tossed tall boys and argued over which guitar player was which on the record. John and Ronnie were across the room sharing some secret, laughing at me and T.J. as if they were fourth graders and we were substitute teachers. Their minds had left them hours ago.

The Allman Brothers were idle, wild, and southern, musically travelling over desert and mountain trails. We listened and talked and travelled with them. T.J. told me a lot of kid stuff, how his father built the cabin when he was seven years old, how he and his brothers would spend the night there when guests were at the main house.

"You're really close to your brother Jeff, aren't you, T.J.?"

"I don't even think of him as a separate person. We're two halves of the same ... whatever."

"That's cool — that togetherness."

"It comes from my father. He's really big on family loyalty. My dad ... is like the biggest force in my life."

"Where's Jeff staying these days?"

"He's living with his girlfriend up in Marblehead. You have any brothers, Pete?"

"Don't ask." I didn't want to think about Malcolm. The police had picked him up in New York driving a stolen van; he was serving his sentence now in Sing Sing.

T.J. smiled at me wearily. We sat quietly for a moment, both in soggy, post-climactic alcoholic stupors. "I think I'll see what's going on in the house," he said after a while.

"Okay. Say hello to Susie for me." I'd been teasing T.J. about Susie Blomberg all summer. T.J. chuckled, then stood up and left, letting the cabin door slam behind him. John and Ronnie finished off the last six-pack. I started to feel dizzy. It was about two o'clock in the morning when I fell asleep.

✹

I woke up on a hard pine bench. The record changer was still playing *Idlewild South* from the night before. Ronnie and John Bragg had already awakened and left. I felt a little nauseated, but not terribly hung over. Inside the cabin was dark; there were only two small, narrow windows. I spent a few minutes exploring the cabin, looking for mementos of T.J.'s childhood, or some evidence of his or his brother's private lives.

On a broad, oaken bureau in the back of the cabin was a photograph of the three Adams children — T.J., Jeffrey, and the oldest brother, Rick. The boys were standing on a dock with fishing gear. Jeff looked about fifteen years old in the photo, Rick Adams about seventeen. That would have made T.J. about twelve, though he looked younger. The gray background of the black-and-white photo was ambiguous; was it foggy or sunny on the day that picture was taken? And who was the cameraman? Of that there was no doubt.

It was their superimposing father, framing his three boys in the photo lens, inspecting his sons, dominating them.

I stared at the photo for a long time, trying to fill in the story. I pretended I didn't know any of these boys, that this was a lone photograph hanging in a once-visited gallery. There was symmetry and sequence in the photo — three boys standing in order of age and descending height — a chain of emulation, metamorphosis of themes. All the same and yet each different. The two older boys were imposing even in this still photo. Rick was plain-faced and robust, stockier and more ordinary than his brothers; he looked squarely through the lens into the photographer's eyes and soul. Jeff was a character study: tossed white hair, young and willful, wispy, freckled smile. Filled with rightness and purpose even when enjoying himself, the roughest and most boyish of the three.

Though T.J. was surely a member of this team, in some uncertain way he seemed not to quite fit in. T.J. looked away from the camera and toward his older brothers with a glow of babyish excitement on his face, but also a trace of trouble, a faint longing for separateness. Did he know even then that he was gay? Did he fear that his father would one day discover his secret?

I lay back down on the bench where I'd slept and tried to stave off an increasing dizziness. Craving solidity, I rested my head on hard wood. The door of the cabin creaked open and T.J. walked in.

"Hello, Thomas Jerrett Adams."

"Hello, Peter Joseph Givens." T.J. and I had taken recently to calling each other by our full names. It made me feel like a special person, and a complete entity.

"DT was great last night, huh," I said.

"Incredible. I wish I could write songs like that."

"I realized something last night. It's a good thing I don't play the guitar."

"But you do play guitar," he said, curiously.

"But I'm not really good. If I was a really good guitarist, that's all I would ever do. I wouldn't go to college, I wouldn't work. I'd just play the guitar and go broke."

"Maybe you'd be famous."

"Yeah, like DT. *'Hey, baby, don't flap your lip on DT, your lover man.'*" DT was a white man with long black hippie hair and wild wolf eyes, who'd accent his songs with bits of Negro vernacular and an exaggerated southern drawl.

"Hey, baby." T.J. mimicked DT's low-down growl. We always imitated DT when we were together. It was our theme song, our private joke.

T.J. was wearing a blue t-shirt and baggy, blue-striped white shorts. He sat in a white wicker chair with one foot lifted onto the seat, one knee tucked between crossed arms, and raked his toes and the ball of his foot over a rip in the wicker. A stream of white sunlight cut across the shadows and fell on a corner of his face and the tip of his knee. I could see dust particles floating slowly in the beam of sunlight, miniscule satellites orbiting some invisible center. T.J. smiled at me silently for a moment, as he often did lately, harboring some private opinion of me, some personal thought he wouldn't share. His orange pekoe eyes gleamed with happiness as they peered peacefully into mine. He rubbed his bottom against the wicker seat; his rectum was tingling, I knew, making its presence known. The sun felt warm in the cabin. T.J. sucked the cool morning freshness through his nostrils into his lungs. He felt good this morning. I could feel it. Lately I thought I could always tell what he was feeling.

I'd been sensing a certain pathos about T.J. because of his degrading affair with Chris Thayer, and because even I had seen him as second-best to Chris. T.J. was a more earthbound, organic creature. Even the colors of his skin, hair, and eyes — all autumnal browns and wood-like shades — had been eclipsed by Chris's regal shower of gold, white, and yellow.

But since the springtime the balance had shifted. T.J. was real. Chris was a ghost. In the end, I would cry when T.J. left me. I would pound my bed with my fists in infantile fury, feel far more than I'd ever felt for Chris, or Cady, or anyone.

I snapped out of my reverie and saw T.J. looking at me, perplexed. I forced a cheery attitude.

"So when's the wedding, T.J.? I already picked out your wedding present. A year's supply of Pampers."

T.J. giggled. He liked it when I teased him about girls, the absurdity of it. "Oh, nothing happened, Pete. We just talked all night." Another boy might have invented a tale of sexual conquest, but T.J. knew how that would upset me.

"Good," I said. "'Cause I would never do something like that to you."

A tense look flashed across T.J.'s face. I thought I had reminded him of the night Chris Thayer screwed Jenny Richards in their room while T.J. covered his head with the blanket and pretended to sleep.

T.J. had told me about it only once. Jenny Richards kept saying, No, what about your roommate? Don't worry about him, Chris insisted. There was silence for a while. T.J. thought they had gone to sleep. But then he could hear they were doing it.

He must have felt so horrible. Just imagine it: Chris absorbed in Jenny's mouth and pussy, Jenny absorbed with Chris's body and sweet, fat sex organ. The sloppy sounds of wet, mushy flesh. Whimpers of submission, Chris's foghorn tenor gasping to climax. And T.J., forgotten in the moment of orgasm, reduced beyond the status of trivia to virtual nonexistence.

Perhaps he watched them do it — breathless, mesmerized by the pornographic thrill of Chris's straining buttocks twisting and shoving under the sheet. Or perhaps he hid beneath his pillow. Somehow I knew what T.J. felt that night. And for some unknown reason, the knowledge felt like memory: girl squeals pierced T.J.'s eardrums like needles; the sounds shot down his spine into his legs; his leg muscles spasmed and his eyelids fluttered, his brain and vision charged with oxygen, his nerves under assault.

"Don't worry, Peter Givens, don't worry," T.J. whispered, more to himself than to me. For the time being, he wanted to be good to me. He passed up his chance to seed my imagination with the terror of bisexual betrayal.

T.J. stood up from the wicker chair. "You want some breakfast, Pete?"

"Sure." We walked out of the cabin and up a short hill to the main house. I started singing in DT's Alabama drawl.

> *"I had a boa constrictor wrapped 'round my neck.*
> *The long black sucker was chokin' me to death.*
> *If I don't die before I wake, I swear to God..."*

T.J. joined me on the chorus:

> *"I'm gonna hang that heavy lovin' Snakelady."*

We sang together like plantation Negroes. T.J. and I were close enough to feel each other's body heat, like radiators. I guess the DT concert was the social event of my life.

✺

Moonshot and John Bragg were in the house when we got there. We crowded into the kitchen and cooked eggs, bacon, English muffins. T.J. made pancakes, really good ones. We sat on the outdoor terrace and stuffed ourselves under the morning sun.

Moonshot interrupted the munching and chomping, his mouth full of English muffin. "So, T.J., when are your parents coming back?"

"My dad's playing in a golf tournament in Old Lyme. They should be back tonight."

I felt a chilled rush at the thought of meeting Mr. Adams. Jerrett William Adams. How could I not be excited? T.J. had talked about his father often: "My father says you can get anything in life if you go after it," "My dad will kill me if I get a C in calculus," or "People are afraid of my father." I couldn't help but be scared myself.

I had come so far from my pointless obsession with Cady Donaldson. From reading about Cady's father in *Who's Who in America* to now, actually meeting T.J.'s dad. From searching on a roadmap for Cady's hometown to spending the night in the cabin where the Adams boys had slept as children. I imagined eight-year-old T.J. playing hide-and-go-seek under the cabin rafters with big brother Jeffrey, who was starting to think this game was silly. I thought of them sleeping together, nestled under blankets on those cool summer nights when their father would let them camp out in the cabin. T.J. loved his brother so much, spoke of him so often. I speculated about incestuous longings, but rejected the thought. Still, their brotherly love was so beautiful it saddened me and thrilled me.

We spent the day swimming at the home of the Peck family, friends of T.J. in Point O' Woods. A beautiful woman in her forties whom I'd met at spring commencement recognized me by the pool and came out to say hello. She told me she was spending August with the Pecks. T.J. acted snooty and affected in front of the Peck sisters by the poolside; I'd never seen him act that way before. I wondered how well I knew him.

※

We drove back to T.J.'s house in the late afternoon. Mrs. Adams was on the back patio preparing hamburgers for dinner. She was wearing a white-spotted dress, and she'd cut her hair short since the last time I'd visited. Seeing her again, I could see Jeff's smile in her nearly skeletal face and the tightly drawn corners of her eyes; the features were more attractive as part of Jeff's sporty, Nordic mystique.

T.J.'s father came out through the screen door. Mr. Adams was wearing a white sports shirt unbuttoned halfway down the chest and beige slacks. He was a tall, full-bodied man; his gene for height had evidently bypassed his children. His arms, tanned to bronze, were covered with curly white hair. He walked first towards Ron, smiling, and shook his hand fondly. "Howdy, Moonshot," he said, his voice a scraping baritone. I hadn't known that Ron had ever been to T.J.'s home before.

Mr. Adams sat in a patio chair next to his wife and crossed his legs at the knee. T.J. sat behind us by the grill, turning burger patties, his legs crossed like his father's. I studied Mr. Adams with an almost primal intensity. This man was the source of my boyfriend's life, I thought. This man had molded T.J. into someone I could love.

He said very little, sipping a martini and smiling to himself while Mrs. Adams talked continuously. (T.J.'s big mouth was obviously inherited from his mother.) My head was still swimming from drinking too much, and her voice faded momentarily to an echo in the background. I could barely make out her speaking to T.J., something about how he ought to try waterskiing, he'd probably like it since he liked downhill. There was pressure in my ears, and then a pop.

Mrs. Adams's voice slipped back into the foreground. "Peter says he wants to go to Webster College, Jerrett." T.J.'s father was an alumnus of my future college.

"Oh, really," Mr. Adams said, glancing over his shoulder to see how the burgers were doing. T.J.'s dad seemed bored and itchy — out of place in his own backyard. He reminded me of a hyperactive child in a rare moment of forced good behavior, deprived of his instincts and not knowing quite how to act or what to say.

"You should hear Pete play the bass, Dad," said T.J. Mrs. Adams reminded her husband of the time he got drunk and played tub bass at a party. Too seriously, I asked how he could control the pitch of a rubber band and broomstick. He smiled and looked downwards, embarrassed perhaps by the memory and by the stupidity of my question.

In the many years since that summer I've learned that intelligent older people develop a heightened awareness, bordering on telepathy, over time. As a transparent sixteen-year-old, I couldn't know what Mr. Adams really thought of me. I'm sure I was staring too intently, as was my habit at that age. I tried to visualize the nights that Jeff and then T.J. were conceived, the exact miraculous instant when their father brought his marvelous children into being. Did Mr. Adams sense my almost predatory fascination with him? Did he think I was just weird, or did he suspect I was sleeping with his son?

He was distantly curious towards me, perhaps inquiring to himself what I was doing in his home. Why were there now two black boys from the ghetto eating hamburgers on his patio? He never looked directly at me; rather his eyes scanned blankly in my direction. He turned to Moonshot and whispered something to him I couldn't hear.

Mrs. Adams put her hand on her husband's thigh, pressing a finger into the muscle. "Jerrett, come inside. I have to ask you something."

"Yes, dear," he said with exaggerated weariness, smiling in Moonshot's direction; I think he even winked at him as he stood up and followed his wife into the house.

T.J. was still turning burgers on the grill. "How many you up for, Moonshot?" he asked.

Moonshot was grinning secretively, chewing on a toothpick. He slouched back and put his foot up on an empty patio chair. "Just keep cooking," he said.

"How about you, Pete?"

I hesitated before answering. Why had T.J. asked Ronnie first? "Two," I murmured. T.J. beamed a smile in my direction.

"Two?" said Moonshot. "I can eat at least five."

Something was burning under my collar. I wasn't sure whether I was angry or tired. I stood up and stretched. "I'm going inside to wash my hands," I said.

"Hurry back. They're almost done," said T.J.

I walked through the screen door and across the living room to the bath. From inside, I could hear T.J.'s parents talking in the kitchen.

"Well, I have to leave next Friday," said Mr. Adams.

"I'll just have to let them know," said his wife. I turned on the water to wash, drowning them out. When I turned the faucet off, I could hear them again.

"Who is this new fellow?" It was Mr. Adams speaking.

"The quiet boy?"

"Right. Not Moonshot, the other one."

"He's been here before. They're very close, apparently."

"Doesn't Tom have any white friends?"

"Of course he does, Jerrett."

"It doesn't seem a little strange to you? Always bringing black people to our house."

"No, it does not seem strange. They're both good boys."

"Well, I like Moonshot. That other one, though. He's got something on his mind."

I was sure I didn't want to hear the rest of this conversation. I dried my hands quickly and hurried back outside. A minute later Mr. and Mrs. Adams came out and we started to eat. I only had one hamburger. Moonshot must have eaten ten.

T.J. was calm and quiet through dinner, adopting his father's strategic aloofness. After dinner, Mr. Adams drove off in his Porsche to his country club. T.J. asked his mother if he could take the air conditioner from the study. When she said no, he abruptly exploded, yelling that he wanted it and that Dad would let him have it. No warning, no precipitous incline to frenzy; just sudden black-scowled infant fury. Was T.J. crazy? I wondered if this was his father's way of meeting resistance, and T.J. was only imitating his dad. Somehow I felt this was not an unusual scene in the Adams house. Mrs. Adams backed down and T.J. loaded the air conditioner into the trunk of his car, his tantrum immediately forgotten. We drove back to Briarwood, arriving on campus about a half hour after dark.

15

That night I had trouble sleeping. I tossed about for an hour, then sat up on my bed and looked out the window. The lawn was shimmering in a mix of black and dark green light. I ran my fingers across the chipped paint on the windowsill and listened to the wind rustling through the trees outside the dorm.

I was thinking about Moonshot. Mr. Adams had liked Ronnie so much better than me. He'd barely acknowledged me, no more than politeness required, but he and Ronnie seemed like old buddies. "Howdy, Moonshot," I kept hearing in my head. When had Moonshot ever been to T.J.'s house?

This jealousy wasn't new. I had always envied Ronnie's personality. He always had T.J. laughing. And it wasn't just comedy. I'd seen them many times having long conversations under a tree on the lawn, or sitting with their backs to the fence on the tennis court, T.J. more peaceful than I'd ever seen him. I'd so often wondered what they were talking about.

I was certain that T.J. liked Ronnie better than me erotically. Who could blame him? At times I thought Moonshot was created in a cauldron by a witch intent on forging a god of sex. He had that freaky, wiry, miscreated body — distorted like an African wood carving. And then, that dick. That construction ball of black flesh swinging over the toilet. It screamed out sex, it affected your brain. When Moonshot walked into the shower, you instinctively felt like bowing before him. How could I compete with black reptilian royalty?

By morning I was delirious with jealousy. Moonshot had fucked my boyfriend. I just knew he'd screwed T.J. It hurt to dwell on it — the sights and the sounds — but I couldn't jettison the thought. I desperately wanted these feelings to go away. My jealousy felt like a permanent wound, like a lost arm or finger. What could I do to fix the situation? There had to be some way.

I knew. I could sleep with Ronnie. It was the only way I could think of to restore my equilibrium. If I could have what T.J. had, if I could know what T.J. felt in Ronnie's bed, that would make us equal again, and everything would be right.

※

T.J. knocked on my door that morning and asked if I wanted to go to breakfast. I said yes, though I felt like a beggar taking alms. As we walked to the dining hall, I kept zigzagging towards and away from him — close enough to feel his warmth, then away to the edge of the path. T.J. didn't notice my ambivalence. He was in a good mood this morning, yapping away about the concert and Susie Blomberg and the summer program kids. I didn't say much, but I was starting to feel a little better. I might have even smiled. I listened as T.J.'s skittering brain sent random thoughts to his mouth in rapid-fire sequence. He was such a screwball, sometimes, I thought. No wonder I loved him so much.

"We haven't been over to Memorial in a while," he said. At least he still wanted to have sex with me. I hadn't been reduced to complete erotic uselessness. Even if I was second-best. My belly was awash with confused feelings.

Moonshot came over and sat with us at breakfast. He slapped T.J. on the back and they both grinned. I became glum and excited at the same time. I felt wet and drained inside. I hated Moonshot. No, I didn't. I couldn't hate Moonshot if T.J. loved him. Ronnie looked beautiful this morning, more beautiful than I'd ever noticed before. Even if he was ugly. I felt righteously beaten. Anyone who could make my boyfriend smile like that deserved my respect. I would accept defeat with grace. Hail to Moonshot the First.

✵

Every evening after dinner Ronnie showered in the dormitory. Most nights I had made a special point to catch the after-dinner show. Tonight I planned to do more than look — I was going to make Moonshot and steal him away from T.J. When I heard the water running, I headed down the hallway with my shaving kit.

I was hyperventilating as I entered the bathroom. Moonshot walked from the shower, dripping wet, feet flopping on the tile, and took a long clear piss in the urinal, expelling the pints of water he drank to keep cool out on the athletic fields. I stood behind him, brushing my teeth, needlessly combing my hair. From the rear view I could see the head of his dick hanging halfway to his kneecaps. My heart slowed as I watched. Moonshot's cock had its own center of gravity; independent of his body, it formed its own gravitational interaction with the earth. I was captivated by its weight, its slow, subtle movements. Ron turned towards the water basin to dry himself. His cock draped itself half-curled over the outer curve of his thigh and got trapped there, too heavy to fall back freely; he had to lift his knee and kick it back over between his legs. (I thought of a sleeping crocodile lying in your path that hesitates, then moodily responds to a kick in its side by moving out of your way, after considering the option of killing and eating you instead.) With each heavy bounce, each lazy, exaggerated dangle, a blast of oxygen shot into my brain.

Ron turned and caught me staring. I lost my nerve. I hurried out of the bathroom and back to my room. A minute later the door opened. Moonshot walked in, nude, carrying his towel balled up in one hand. "Stop fucking around with me, Pete."

I could feel the outstretched fingers of invisible hands, touching lightly at the back of my head, then pressing forwards, the fingers coming to right angles with the palms, pushing my head forwards and downwards. And a silent command: "Fall on your knees, love him and serve him. Suck like a slave."

Every now and then, an unexpected experience gives us an empirical understanding of nature; I knew firsthand how the field mouse feels when cornered by the giant rattler, paralyzed by its hiss and its stare.

※

I didn't feel any better after making it with Moonshot. If anything, I felt worse. Moonshot was incredible. So much man, you just wanted to crawl into the cracks in the floor. I couldn't compete with him for T.J. and I knew it.

I felt sick and tight inside. I was awfully depressed. And of course, I saw T.J. and Moonshot together everywhere. Coming from the swimming pool, driving off campus. Playing volleyball with Susie and Meg, laughing, laughing. Hahahahahaha. Goddammit! Why was it so hard to keep my boyfriend to myself?

Finally I couldn't stand it. I went to see T.J. in his room. "Why do you like Moonshot more than me?" I demanded. I felt like stamping my foot on the floor, but I didn't.

"Are you menstruating or something? You're so paranoid about Lewis."

"Answer my question, T.J."

"Okay. I'll tell you. Ron's got his head more together than you do. He knows who he is, you don't."

"What are you talking about?"

"Ronnie has soul. I like soul. You're an Uncle Tom."

"I can't believe you'd say something like that right to my face."

"I'm not saying I don't like you, Peter. I like you a lot. You don't know Ronnie. You never talk to him. Moonshot is really cool. He's deep. And that dick — it's like Dracula. 'Come to me,' it says."

"So what about Chris Thayer?" I was trying to get revenge.

"What about him?"

Right. What about him? I thought fast and made something up. "He's nothing like Ronnie. He's the exact opposite."

T.J. leaned back and crossed his legs. He thought for a moment. "Now I'm starting to figure you out. You thought I was in love with Chris, and if you acted like Chris I'd fall in love with you."

That made sense, but it wasn't what I was thinking. "Are you in love with me?" I asked.

T.J. paused. "Sort of."

"I don't act like anybody. I act like myself."

"Then what are you bitching about?"

"I hate Moonshot. I'm gonna kill him. You better get it while you can, 'cause I'm gonna kill his ass."

"He'll have you on your knees in two seconds. You don't fool me."

"What?"

T.J. laughed. "He told me about you. You're not jealous because Ron is getting me, you're jealous because I'm getting Ronnie."

"I hate you, T.J. I'm gonna kill you and Moonshot."

"Jesus, Pete. I think it's time to change your Tampax."

"Stop making fun of me."

"I'm sorry. But I've never seen you act like this before."

I stood there, staring at T.J. in thoughtless silence. I felt something pushing at me, rushing me, a hard compulsion, and I blurted it out. "I love you, T.J. I'm crazy about you. I'm completely destroyed with love for you."

T.J. looked at me for the longest while. I didn't say a word. "Come here," he said finally.

I walked over and stood next to his bed.

"Sit down." I sat and T.J. put his arm around my shoulder.

"I've been in love with you forever, Peter. I was in love with you on Bennett's corridor. But I knew you weren't in love with me." He pinched some of my hair between his fingers and tugged through the knotted nap. It hurt and I winced. T.J. smiled and put his hand back in his lap. He went on talking.

"And then when Chris came to school, you acted all crazy over him. So I gave up on you. We were still friends, and we were making it. I figured that's all you wanted."

"But you wanted more?"

"You see, I always thought I was going to get married someday. Like my dad and mom. They have a good marriage. That was the biggest thing in my life when I was a kid, a close family. Me and Jeff and Rick, and my parents. But then I realized I was never going to get married. I just didn't like girls enough. Partly because I was in love with you, I realized I was one hundred percent gay. Then my future became — just this big question mark. What does it really mean to be queer? What about love, all that kind of stuff. Where does that fit in? I think I needed a boyfriend just for the sake of having one. I had to know that was a part of being gay. And if it wasn't going to be you, then maybe it could be Chris, I thought."

"Or Moonshot?"

"Right."

"I was never in love with Chris, T.J. Not really. I was just starstruck because his family was famous. Now I think he's a jerk."

"I was kind of mad at you for a while, because I thought you had turned me totally gay."

"But I didn't seduce you. You seduced me."

"I don't mean sexwise. I mean emotionally."

This was a complete surprise. You never do know what people are thinking.

T.J. put his arm back around my shoulder. "Anyway, no matter how I feel about Chris or Ronnie, you're my boyfriend from now on. You and I have the right fit. The way you and I get along, that's the way my dad and mom get along."

"Which one am I? Your mother or your dad?"

T.J. smiled to himself and didn't answer right away. "I didn't mean it that literally."

"I wish you could get me pregnant," I said.

"I wish you could get *me* pregnant."

"No, I wish you could get *me* pregnant."

"Well, we'll just have to keep trying until one of us gets pregnant."

"Okay. Me first."

"No, me first."

"No, *me* first."

"I want a divorce," said T.J.

That did it. T.J. had hit my funny bone with a ball-head hammer. When I stopped laughing, I snuggled in close to his chest. His body felt like a magic rock, giving off vibrations like a lodestone. I wasn't sure whether I should speak or not, so I didn't say anything.

※

We sat together like that for at least an hour. T.J. was very quiet. I finally calmed down. T.J. got up and went out to Mr. Hays's apartment and brought back two Budweisers.

"Pete, you want a beer?"

"Sure." He tossed me a tall boy and sat down on the bed. There was silence for a minute. I glanced at the window. "How's your air conditioner working?" I asked.

"Fine." He shrugged and shook his head, dismissing the subject.

210

"I wish I had one. I got two choices, either open the window and die from mosquitoes or close the window and die from the heat."

T.J. was in a still, spacious mood now. He seemed unsure of me, unsure of what he had said to me. Something was on his mind, and I still had some questions to ask him. I got up, closed the door, and sat back down on the bed.

"T.J., do you think you'll ever make up with Chris Thayer?"

"Nope."

"But you want to, right?"

"Chris likes girls."

"You sure?"

He paused. "Yeah."

I thought for a second. "Your parents are really cool."

"Yeah, I dig my dad. People are scared of him."

"Does he ever let you drive his Porsche?"

T.J. gulped down a swig of Budweiser. "Hell no, Pete."

The pace of this conversation was odd. What was T.J. thinking about? I doubled back, prodded further. "Chris is crazy. He's the real Uncle Tom. A gay Uncle Tom."

"He changed a lot. I had a bad dream about him."

"Oh yeah?" I got excited. "Tell me about it. I'll analyze your dream for you."

T.J. described a hospital room with a bed and a table with a vase of yellow flowers. Chris Thayer lay in the bed with his back in a cast. His back was broken. T.J. came into the room to visit Chris. The two of them were talking. Suddenly Chris jumped up in the bed and cursed at T.J. ("You little shit! You little shit!") Then the whole room turned slantways and started shaking. T.J. could see the entire hospital room, with him and Chris in it, inside a giant glass cube, tumbling down a hill. Chris fell out of the bed on top of T.J. T.J. couldn't get out from under Chris, while the cube turned somersaults down the hill until T.J. woke up.

"I could win the Nobel Prize for psychoanalyzing you, T.J. For figuring out your brain, I definitely would deserve to win something. Now, don't get alarmed. Basically, that dream means you're crazy. When you saw the room in a cube rolling down the hill, that's an image of rolling dice, which means you're gambling your life away. No, it means you're shooting craps with your life, and you think your life is crap. Also, you want to kill Chris Thayer. No, you want Chris to break his back so he can't get it up with girls anymore. That's what it really means." I was working T.J.'s nerves.

"Bullshit, Pete. You could win the Nobel Prize for psychosis, not for psychoanalysis."

T.J. stood up from the bed and looked out the window. We could hear a radio playing Creedence Clearwater Revival (*"O Suzie Q, O Suzie Q, honey, I love you"*). Two boys and girls were laughing out on the lawn. T.J. stood still watching for a while, then came back and sat down on my bed.

"When I first met Chris he was really cool and funny. Except sometimes he was kind of pathetic. He'd just sit there staring into space for no reason. I felt sorry for him."

"He's really cute, I have to admit. He reminds me of Huckleberry Finn. I know what you mean about him staring into space."

"I liked being his roommate. But he changed. He ended up being kind of an asshole. Even before he squealed on me."

"What do you mean?"

"Things like throwing his clothes around the room, making me clean it up. Making fun of me sometimes, in front of people." T.J. paused for a moment, looked down towards the floor. "You think you know Chris, Pete, but you don't." Chris had said the same thing to me about T.J. Did I know anybody? Did I have any idea what was going on?

"I know he fucks girls, but I'm sure he likes boys too. In the shower sometimes, he was totally obvious. Playing with his dick with the soap and stuff like that." T.J.'s eyes brightened.

"Did you hear about that guy that popped a hard-on in the shower? Wow!" Mark Fix had lost control of himself after a baseball game. I didn't believe Mark was gay, but the story had spread through school.

"Embarrassing," I said. "That's why I keep my hand on the cold water faucet."

"I wonder who made him pop a hard-on. I'll bet it was Billy Green." Billy was a hunky, straight-haired brunet and the captain of the lacrosse team. T.J. and I both liked Billy Green, and we always joked about having sex with him.

"Could you imagine if Moonshot popped a hard-on in the shower? He'd knock the whole gymnasium down. All these naked guys would come running out of the gym screaming."

"Right. Like in the monster movies. Like in *The Blob* when all those people come running out of the theater."

"Moonshot Lewis," I said. "A legend in his own time."

"That's for sure," said T.J., shaking his head slowly.

I loved talking queer talk with T.J. It felt great, being so open and relaxed about it. T.J. stood up and put on his shoes.

"Pete, let's go over to Memorial."

※

It was too dangerous to have sex in our dormitory, so T.J. and I always walked across the main lawn to Memorial Building, the biggest and oldest dormitory on campus. We took a room on the top floor, on the front side of the building so we could hear if anyone came through the front door. The only likely visitors were the security guard, who knew us and wouldn't bother us (unless he caught us cornholing) or some of the straight kids sneaking in to ball their girlfriends.

Inside the building was dark, except for the red fire switch lights. We didn't dare turn on a light. In the moonlight coming through the window the edges of T.J.'s skin looked literally white. We lay down on an unsheeted mattress and took our clothes off. First we hugged and french-

213

kissed. ("I love you, Peter." "I love you, T.J.") T.J.'s tongue fiddled in my mouth like a goldfish flopping in a quarter inch of water. Then I bent him over and fucked him. The wooden bed frame creaked as if it were going to crack. T.J. let out breathy little hoots with each pump from my hips. I loved those little hoots; I thought I owned them. If he missed one, I got angry and pounded him harder, driving his face into the headboard until I heard the helpless yelping that satisfied me.

I knew Moonshot had been there. I could feel him inside of T.J. I imagined the wall of T.J.'s ass stretched to threads by Ronnie's dick, T.J.'s eyes pirouetting in delirium. And the sounds. The sounds of dead lungs exploding back to life. The muffled cries of T.J. — little T.J., my brown-eyed baby love — releasing his voice, his only link to sanity, while Ronnie saturated him with shattering pain. And I could see Moonshot fumbling, struggling to be gentle, half regretting his gift of enormity, trying to love T.J. with his dick. But all he could do was hurt him.

It was a stabbing, stinging image, mixed with pain and excitement. I still hated the thought, but I knew it had happened and I knew I would have to live with it.

After we fucked, I brought T.J. off with a blowjob. We lay still for a short while, then sat up and continued our silly boy-lover gabbing.

"Why don't you ball Susie, T.J.? You know she needs your nuts."

"Susie is frigid. She's not giving it up to nobody."

"Excuses, excuses. You're just a faggot. You could ball her if you wanted to."

"Look whose talking. I don't see you dating any girls."

"You *quee-eeeer.*" T.J. threw his dirty socks in my face.

I moved closer and rested my head in T.J.'s lap. "I overheard your father talking about me. He said I was a weirdo."

"He did?" T.J. was silent for a moment. "That's just because you're so quiet. You were a mystery to him."

"I freaked out over it."

T.J. was scraping his fingernails in my hair, pinching little bits of it and tugging. "We'll go out sometime. I'll help you break the ice with him." He paused. "I know you need help breaking the ice." He stopped playing with my hair. We lay silently for several minutes.

"Do you ever dream about me, Pete?"

"I don't have to dream about you, T.J. You're real. I'll dream about you after we graduate."

"I'll come and visit you in college," he promised. And he did.

※

It was August, and the summer program was winding down. The days were passing too quickly. T.J. heard that he'd been accepted off the waiting list at St. Christopher's. I was terribly upset by the news. I'd been expecting to spend our senior year together as roommates and lovers. I slunk around for several days and refused to talk to him.

After a week my anger passed, and I wanted to talk to T.J. again. St. Christopher's wasn't the end of the world. We could write and visit on vacations, and then after we graduated we could go to the same college. It excited me to think of my relationship with T.J. spanning not just months, but years.

I stood in T.J.'s doorway and mumbled something inaudible, like "How you doing?"

"Are you still mad at me?"

"No," I said.

"Come in and sit down."

I came in and sat on the windowsill. T.J. sat up on his bed.

"I can't come back here, Pete. I don't ever want to see Thayer anymore. And all the suspicious looks people were giving me."

"Was it really that bad?"

"Yes!" he said with sudden intensity. "I'd go into the shower after tennis practice and everybody would go to the other end of the shower. At one of my matches, somebody told my opponent. After I beat him he told me he doesn't shake hands with queers."

"I didn't know about all that." I felt sick at the thought of my king dethroned by prejudice.

"Anyway, Dean Press advised me to transfer."

"I hate Dean Press."

"We'll still see each other, Pete. I promise."

I crossed my arms and tried to look as pitiable and dejected as possible. T.J. stared at me sweetly for a moment.

"Pete, take a ride with me, okay?"

※

T.J. and I had rented bicycles for the summer. We rode down the hill, across Route 9, and through the woods. When we came to the railroad tracks, I asked T.J. where we were going.

"There's an incredible cliff about a half mile from here." We walked our bikes over the tracks and rode down a bumpy dirt path through the bushes. The path became less and less passable, crisscrossed with tree roots and studded with rocks. At one point, T.J. said we had to get off our bikes and walk. "You don't want to be on a bike this close. You might lose control and ride off the cliff." The dirt trail came to an end in a tangle of blueberry hedges. We pushed through the bushes and found a spread of flat land. The clearing ended at a straight drop-off. From the hedges, I couldn't see beyond the drop. I stopped, but T.J. walked on.

"What are you afraid of?" he said.

"What's out there?"

"Come look. You can see the whole river from here."

I wasn't close to the edge. The clearing was thirty yards to the cliff. Still, I was nervous. I took a few steps and stopped.

"Come on, Peter." T.J. was now standing on the edge of the cliff.

My whole body had come alive with fear. Even the air frightened me. The wind was blowing across the clearing, scattering sand and dust. The bushes behind me were rustling. The sun was crashing down on the clearing in full brightness, so that the sand was gleaming gold and bits of quartz were sparkling in the grass. T.J. had sat down in a squat. He rested his rump on the ground and then slowly stretched out his legs. He shunted forward inch by inch until his legs were hanging over the cliff. I wanted to call to him to be careful, but I was afraid of startling him.

He sat there looking out over the valley. I came closer and stopped again. T.J. looked over his shoulder. "Pete, you're not going to fall off from ten feet away."

I walked until I was standing right behind him. He pointed off to the north. "You can follow the river until it disappears into the mountains."

"Aren't you scared, T.J.?"

"Shitless," he said. "I like it." He pointed to the south. "Through that gap there, that's the interstate. That's the road I drive home on."

I got down on my knees and edged closer. I was terrified, but not so much of falling off. It was more like I was infused with cosmic fear. The sensations I felt inside were pressing out against my skin, like air inside a balloon. Here I was, on this tiny, airborne sand bar, where the forest had stopped growing for some unknown reason, looking out over the enormous valley.

"You couldn't really fall off here," T.J. said. "It would be an incredibly spastic thing to do. There's no guarantee, I mean it could happen, but you have to believe you're not going to spaz out with your whole life on the line. If you spaz out with your life at stake — that's pathetic. I couldn't live with that much self-doubt. I just couldn't get what I want out of life."

I inched my legs towards the edge until my feet were just hanging over. I was exhilarated with fear.

"Close your eyes," T.J. said.

"No way."

"Just for a minute." T.J. was sitting with his eyes squeezed shut. I closed my eyes, and my body came even more alive with blindness. It was as though I could feel the entire valley inside of me, the entire vast expanse, the course of the river, the mass of the hills, had been captured in my body, like in a little bottle. I felt electricity under my fingernails, blood pumping in my neck, the wind nipping at my face. My eardrums felt like wind tunnels.

"How you doing?" T.J. said.

"Okay." I opened my eyes and he was looking at me. He turned to look out again and closed his eyes. I sat there for a moment watching my boyfriend, watching him breathe. He squeezed his eyes even tighter.

"This is life," he whispered.

※

Being gay in boarding school had turned my biological calendar upside down. Most students couldn't wait for summer or holiday vacations. I could never wait for vacation to end, to get back to my boyfriends. But this summer had been different. Now that I had fallen in love with T.J., I anticipated the end of the summer program with terror. I felt as though I were on death row; the minutes of my last few days with T.J. passed like the last few minutes of life.

I had difficulty breathing. I alternated between gloom and hyperactive irritation. Everyone noticed, including T.J., who couldn't figure what was wrong. "Pete, you look so bored," he said with disapproval as I lay stunned and withered on my bed. I wondered why T.J. wasn't as depressed as I was.

On the last morning, we had graduation ceremonies for the summer program kids from Hartford. My favorite student in the program got angry at me for not giving him an award in music class. I had to admit he deserved one, I was just distracted.

After the ceremonies I helped T.J. pack his belongings in his car — tennis racquet, stereo speakers, air conditioner. My mind was overloaded with static; I had motor capacity but little more. My allotment of minutes was now down to seconds. T.J. was cool, happy to be leaving. He would spend the rest of the summer playing golf and tennis in Point O' Woods. In the fall he'd go to St. Christopher's for his senior year. I was headed to New York and then back to Briarwood.

T.J. was half smiling now as he shoved a box under the car seat with his foot; he'd realized I was distraught over his leaving. I thought I had a few more minutes, but he looked up at me suddenly. "That's it!" He took two steps towards me, hand outstretched, shook my hand. He held it warmly for a moment. "I'll see you around, Pete." He got into his car, closed the door, drove around the main lawn, down the hill, away.

Somewhere I'd read that if you keep stepping half the distance to a wall, you'd never get to that wall, just each time halfway there, halfway there. I imagined disappearing into a twilight world of microspace, the wall reshaped into bizarre dimensions as I approached infinity. I tried this technique as the end approached, dividing time intervals in half to forestall death forever, but I couldn't cut the instants finely enough. The last whole micron of time leapfrogged over me like an ocean wave, knocked me down, and swept me under.

I began to cry. I ran up the dormitory stairs to my room. John Bragg and Moonshot saw me; I'm sure they knew I was crying about T.J. I threw myself on my bed, pounded the pillows, and kicked my legs in fury. I cried like a half-year-old infant.

I left the dormitory and walked out past the football fields, my eyes still filmed with water. I saw parts of the school campus I'd never seen, but heard about. Senior faculty houses with lovely colored gardens. Fields of tall, yellow grass where criminal students went to smoke pot, where Sean Landport had been caught once screwing a girl. I sobbed and sobbed for T.J. My chest hurt from crying, but I was proud that I could feel so intensely.

I walked until I came to a roadway. I recognized where I was now — near downtown Green River. I went to the downtown malt shop and had a cheeseburger and milkshake. Then I hitched a ride back to school. I'd walked about three miles. I can hold it together, I thought to myself. I'm not going to die.

※

In the late afternoon the day T.J. left Briarwood, Ashley Downer came onto the campus to visit. He said hello to me, forgetting the trouble between us. I had forgotten it, too. Ashley had changed since the Third Form. He wore his hair longer now, until it curled, and he dressed less conservatively. In his new wire-rimmed glasses, dusty jeans, and pointy boots he struck a mixed posture of scholar and rebel. I looked at him and realized how long it had been since our freshman year.

Ashley offered to drive me into Hartford so I could catch a train back to New York. I threw my duffel bag into the backseat of his Volkswagen and we left. The campus was empty and quiet. I could hear a few birds singing, their voices echoing off trees. The sun glared off the main lawn. I felt the hot, gold reflection as we drove around the quad. Then we were covered by the shade of the trees along the winding road. We drove down the hill and away.

Ashley's father had died the year before. Strangely enough, he wanted to talk about it. The experience had changed him, he said. When his father was ill, he had told Ashley that he loved him. For the first time he'd used the actual words. Ashley was chattering away in some mystical manner, about life and the spirit and love and whatnot. He was getting a little boring. I thought that I liked him better as a bigot. I tuned him out and just nodded in the pauses. The sun was gleaming off the dashboard and I couldn't see. I couldn't hear or see. And I didn't want to. T.J. was gone, halfway back to Point O' Woods by now, and I didn't know when I'd see him again.

✸

It's sad for me to end this book. Someday I might write another one. If you're interested in what happened to T.J. and me, I'll tell you just a little. After T.J. graduated from St. Christopher's, he went to college in London. He wrote me letters, though, and told me all about the English. Well, I don't think he told me everything. I know there was a fellow with hazel eyes, but I don't know the details. I went off to college and majored in chemistry. I spent some years that weren't so good. When T.J. came back stateside, he bought a house in Dutchess County. I moved in five years ago, and that's where I am now. I can even see the Rip Van Winkle Bridge from my window.

He's different, of course, not *quite* so wild anymore. I call him Jerrett now. I always liked that name better. That's him in the next room, as a matter of fact, setting the table for dinner. I think I just heard him drop a plate. Sometimes he can still be a bonehead.

If you should happen to see him, don't tell him I said that. It's never any fun when he's mad at me.

Other books of interest from
ALYSON PUBLICATIONS

REFLECTIONS OF A ROCK LOBSTER, by Aaron Fricke, $7.00. Aaron Fricke made national news when he sued his school for the right to take a male date to the prom. Here is his story of growing up gay in America.

ONE TEENAGER IN TEN, edited by Ann Heron, $5.00. One teenager in ten is gay. Here, 26 young people from around the country discuss their coming-out experiences. Their words will provide encouragement for other teenagers facing similar experiences.

IN THE LIFE, edited by Joseph Beam, $9.00. In black slang, the expression "in the life" often means "gay." In this anthology, black gay men from many backgrounds describe their lives and their hopes through essays, short fiction, poetry, and artwork.

BROTHER TO BROTHER, edited by Essex Hemphill, $9.00. Black activist and poet Essex Hemphill has carried on in the footsteps of the late Joseph Beam (editor of *In the Life*) with this new anthology of fiction, essays, and poetry by black gay men.

GOLDENBOY, by Michael Nava, $9.00. When a young man is accused of committing murder to keep his gayness a secret, Henry Rios agrees to defend him. Will new murders, suicide, and a love affair keep Rios from proving his client's innocence?

THE MEN WITH THE PINK TRIANGLE, by Heinz Heger, $8.00. Thousands of gay people suffered persecution at the hands of the Nazi regime. Of the few who survived the concentration camps, only one ever came forward to tell his story. This is his riveting account of those nightmarish years.